BEVERLEY GREEN'S FIRST ADVENTURE

BOOK ONE OF THE BEVERLEY GREEN ADVENTURES

ANDREA C. NEIL

Sign up for the AceWrites Newsletter to receive exclusive content and more – acneil.com/newsletter

For the muses

ONE

"Are you getting enough fiber in your diet? Because things like that are important as you get older, you know." I couldn't see my mom's face over the phone, but I could hear the stern expression in the silence that followed her words. "Are you still there? Beverley?"

I looked at the half-eaten veggie omelet and bowl of fruit on the kitchen table in front of me. A typical weekday breakfast, as healthy as all get-out. But I couldn't help myself—I grabbed a junk mail flyer off the kitchen table, leaned over toward my phone, and crinkled the paper next to the speaker. "I just checked the wrapper of my fried pie; it says there's half a gram of fiber in it."

My mom. The only person who could successfully treat a forty-something daughter like she was both eight and eighty at the same time. She also had an uncanny knack for calling me at the most inconvenient times, like first thing on a Monday morning while I was trying to get ready for work.

"Beverley Green, don't tell me you are eating a fruit pie for breakfast."

"Okay."

"I hear you rolling your eyes," she said with more than a hint of disapproval.

I rolled my eyes and took one last bite of my omelet before giving up on it. I wasn't late for work yet, but I had a feeling this phone call was a harbinger of chaos. I looked around the kitchen for a container to hold my uneaten food; I'd take it to work as a mid-morning snack. "Is there something specific you needed, or did you really call to talk about roughage?"

"Can't I call to say hi?"

Of course she could. But she was doing it all the time these days. She'd never been this nosy during the twenty-plus years I had lived in New York, but now that I was back in Oklahoma, she was all up in my business on a regular basis.

"I'm running late, Mom." I wasn't, but she didn't need to know that.

"You're the boss. You can be late anytime you want," she argued.

I laughed. "No I can't! What if someone was super excited about buying a book this morning, and they got to the shop at ten sharp, and it was still closed? Then they would be sad, and even worse, they might complain." And lord knew I didn't need anyone else complaining about my new bookstore. I slid the rest of my omelet and fruit into a glass storage dish and poured my freshly brewed coffee into a stainless steel to-go cup covered in hipster stickers that said things like, *Boss Babe* and *Hustle All Day*. My new best friend in town had bought them for me as an ironic joke. I loved them.

"Oh. I see your point," she conceded. "All right, I'll let you go then. Just be sure to be nice to everybody, okay? You know how it is, being a new face in a small town. You need to make some friends."

As much as I wanted to tell her not to worry about that particular point, I couldn't. I was worried about it too. And I most certainly did know what it was like being a new face in a small town. Moving to a new city could be trying under the best of circumstances, and gaining acceptance in a close-knit town like Guthrie could be even more tricky. So far I was holding my own, all things considered. But it had been an uphill battle.

"I'm trying, Mom," I said.

I gazed out the window above the kitchen sink, about to launch into a philosophical discourse about the perils and perks of small-town life. But instead, I was speechless. What I saw out that window would have caused me to drop my plate, had I not just put it down.

"Great googly moogly!" I said, by way of philosophical discourse.

"Beverley? Are you okay? Is someone trying to break in? I'll call the police!"

"I gotta go, there are chickens everywhere!" I looked around frantically for my shoes.

"What, did they explode?"

I didn't answer as I ran around the back half of the house like a chicken with its head—like someone looking for her shoes.

"Beverley Green, are you listening to me? What is going on?"

I spotted my Vans and shoved my feet into them. I always kept the laces tied loosely so I could easily slide into my shoes—I was always prepared for emergencies such as this. It was also part of my core value system: tying shoes was a huge existential time suck.

"Everything's fine. But I think the chickens got out of the coop. I need to get off the phone."

"Oh my lord. I told you being a chicken farmer was not a good idea! How are you going to make friends when you're covered with bird poop?"

"Have a great day, Mom, bye!" I dropped my phone on the table and ran out the back door.

It appeared that the chickens had gotten out sometime

while I was eating breakfast, because they'd been fine when I'd checked on them before my meal. I wasn't sure how it had happened, but I could guess. And I guessed it was all Beryl's fault.

Beryl was a large, rust-colored Catalana chicken who was the ringleader of the bird gang I kept in my backyard. Unbeknownst to me at the time of purchase, she had been voted "hen most likely to incite a riot" by her peers, and she wore the title with pride. She hadn't yet pecked my face off, but that was only because of my hyper-vigilance. I knew she was trouble, but I hadn't realized exactly how crafty she was until she started mysteriously escaping from the coop.

The first time it happened, I figured I'd accidentally left the latch off the pen. But the second, third, and fourth times I began to suspect trickery on Beryl's part. She was always the one who would wander the farthest. She must have figured out how to pick (or was that peck?) open the latch of the pen and, in order to satisfy her wanderlust, had flown the coop. Maybe she needed to feel the late-summer Oklahoma breeze on her wattle. Regardless, the hen was gone and I was now going to be very late for work.

Most of the other birds were nowhere to be seen, but a few still milled around the backyard, content to stay behind and hold down the fort. Pearl and Gert, the gentlest girls. They must have waved goodbye to their friends and asked them to send a few postcards. I chased them down easily and put them back in the pen. Then I ran out the backyard and onto the driveway, where I discovered a trail of chickens leading down the street. I started to panic.

If I didn't play this right, I was in danger of losing some of my hens to dogs, cats, or hungry neighbors who might be under the false impression I was giving away free chicken dinners. I knew Beryl would be the one who had made it the farthest from home. Maybe it would be best if I just let her have her freedom... but no. I wanted everyone home safe and sound, even the head rabble rouser.

I stood still for a few seconds, trying to come up with a plan. It occurred to me that this was not quite the picture of domestic bliss I'd envisioned when I'd decided to give up my cushy editing job in New York City earlier in the year, in favor of small-town livin'. In hindsight I'd had an overly simplistic idea of what it would be like. I had naively thought that owning chickens would be romantic, in the way you'd expect someone from a big city to fall for the idea of animal husbandry. Now I was paying for my mistakes. Oh well. There'd be plenty of time for self-admonishment later—right now I needed to wrangle me some chickens.

I started after the ones closest to the house, but they used their avian ESP and scattered in different directions as soon as I got within six feet. I thought about the expression, "like herding cats." For all intents and purposes, cats had nothing on these chickens. I cursed under my breath that my mom had been right —I was about to be covered in bird poop.

It took two pounds of organic grapes and some very fancy kitchen scraps to get everyone except for Beryl rounded up and back in the pen. I finally caught up with her about a block away from Division Street, the main drag leading to downtown. I couldn't catch her outright; instead I had to use reason to try to convince her that no one was going to give her better snacks than me. Finally, after I promised to give her an extra serving of oatmeal upon her safe return, she came along peacefully and joined her sisters in the chicken coop.

I tossed in one last round of treats (including the afore-promised oatmeal) and changed out of my chicken-poop-laden pants. I left them on the porch, saving that problem for another time. I wish I knew what had made those birds wait till I was carrying them to become incontinent. Could they be that vindictive? Or maybe they had great comedic timing. I might never know. Boss or no boss, now I really was late.

After cleaning up, triple-checking the lock on the coop, and grabbing my book bag, I took off for work. I didn't have time to walk to work today, even though I tried to use my car as little as possible. I drove with the windows down, because it was a relatively nice day and I wanted to take advantage of the decreasing humidity.

The sunshine was becoming a little weaker as fall approached, and I could sense fall hiding right around the corner. The temperature might be changing but one thing would always stay the same—the incessant prairie breeze, which whipped my hair everywhere even as the car rolled to a stop at the intersection of Division and Oklahoma. I made a mental note to keep hair ties in the car as I pulled strands of curls out of my eyes. A black SUV pulled up next to me, and on a whim I decided to wave at the driver, since I was feeling all the small-town happy feels. But when I looked over, all I saw was a door handle. Trucks sure were big in the country, I mused.

I laughed as the light turned green and the SUV roared off, leaving me in the proverbial dust. I rarely saw trucks like that in New York City. You'd have a hard time trying to park one, let alone maneuver it through traffic. It was those little—or in this case, huge—differences between New York and Guthrie that I noticed almost every day. A part of me still couldn't believe I'd moved back to Oklahoma, after over twenty years on the East Coast.

It had happened on a whim, or so it seemed to everyone else. But to me, it felt like the logical next step. I woke up the morning after my forty-fifth birthday about six months ago, and realized the only other living thing in my apartment besides me was a half-dead succulent. And that poor thing was about to permanently cross over to the other side.

I'd been successful at work and could hold my own when it came to socializing, but so far I hadn't gotten the romance thing right. Suddenly, on that post-birthday morning, through my hangover goggles, nothing about my life looked right. So I quit my job, threw out the succulent (after giving it a proper memorial service), and gave away all my business suits save one. Then I hauled my books and my ass back to my home state.

And here I was, driving to the bookstore that I owned and operated all by myself. I'd only been open a few months, but I was making it work. And it felt great.

I pulled up in front of my shop, aptly called the Book Store, and checked the time. I was seven minutes late. Not bad, considering the morning's kerfuffle, and I felt pretty good about things, until I noticed who was standing outside the shop in front of the large picture window. Leona Tisdale, my ornery landlady.

Leona was in her early seventies or thereabouts, and favored floral-print dresses with shiny purses that matched her shiny blocky heels. Today's dress was no exception; it featured small white flowers on a dark-blue background. Her shoes and purse matched the flowers and she even had a dark-blue headscarf on, to combat the wind. She was ornery, but I had to admit she was always put together.

She stood ramrod straight with her arms crossed in front of her body, and glared at me. She looked so intimidating I wanted to stay in the car for the rest of the day, but I knew she was waiting for me. Begrudgingly I gathered my things and headed toward her.

"Good morning!" I said with as much fake enthusiasm as I could muster—which wasn't much.

"You're late," she snapped. I was pretty sure she'd meant *Good morning, Beverley, dear!* but had experienced a variety of brain fart that temporarily prevented civility. Honestly though, if she had been nice, I'd have lost my balance because it would have meant the earth had fallen off its axis.

"Yes, I uh, I had a bit of a mishap on the way to work, I'm sorry." I unlocked the front door and went in first to switch on the lights for her.

"Not the best way to run a business," she mumbled, following me in.

"Yes, well. I'm here now. What can I help you with?" Leona wasn't the kind of person that stopped by simply to say hello. In fact, most of the time her visits portended some sort of doom—the question was what variety it would be. My anxiety level started to rise, like it did every time we were in the same room. I was on high alert, feeling trapped.

She looked down at a book on one of the new release tables. It was a trade paperback copy of a new romance novel. The cover depicted a bare-chested beast of a man embracing a well-endowed waif of a woman. As Leona realized what she was looking at, her face pursed like she'd eaten an entire lemon.

"I came by to tell you that someone will be here tomorrow to check the roof leak you complained about."

"I complained about it because there really is a roof leak," I said, setting my bag down behind the counter and turning the computer on. "It's in the back of the store."

"No one else in the building has reported any problems. Just you." She turned her lemon-eating countenance my way. I could tell she didn't believe me, or figured I was exaggerating.

"Would you like to see the bucket full of smelly water I collected underneath the exact spot where the leak is located?" I offered.

She glared at me for a second, sizing me up. "If you hear someone walking around on the roof later, that's what it is."

"Thank you for sending someone out to fix it," I said.

"You're welcome, dear." Leona sighed and took a long look

around the shop. For a brief second the scowl softened, and I hoped she was about to say goodbye and leave the store. Instead, she stood where she was. Darnit. "One more thing," she said.

Oh no. Here it was. I knew what was coming next, and all my muscles tightened up for the energetic car wreck I was about to experience. Since I couldn't hit the brakes, I braced for a collision.

She looked down at the romance book again and pointed at it. "You're not selling any porn again, are you?"

I wanted to smack my forehead in frustration. Or better yet, I wanted to smack her forehead in frustration. "Leona, can't we get past this?"

"Well..." She put her hands on her hips.

It had all started right after I signed the lease for my new store. Due to some very unfortunate misinformation, Leona had managed to get it into her small-town mind that I was opening up a *porn shop* instead of a *book shop*. Don't ask me how someone could make a mistake like that, because I was still trying to figure that one out. I'd tried everything short of flow charts to explain to her that no, it was a regular bookstore, not an adult bookstore. But for the life of me, I could not persuade her otherwise, and she'd tried to evict me before I'd even opened.

My attorney Kelly Passicheck's legal expertise prevailed, however, and I got to keep the space. Because it was all a load of hooey. It was a plain ol' bookstore, for the love of all things nerdy!

When Leona realized she couldn't get me out legally, she'd tried another angle. She and a few other fellow senior citizen conspirators attempted to scare me out by leaving some badly misspelled graffiti on my windows, and once they even broke in and caused a little destruction of property. They were so bad at being bad, however, that Kelly and I managed to catch them in the act once, and we all came to an "agreement." Which consisted of her not slandering me, and me not pressing vandalism charges. I had to hand it to Leona, her technique was entertaining, but ultimately ineffective. But it didn't stop her from holding a grudge. And here we were.

"You're always welcome to take a look around the store," I offered, knowing by now that she wouldn't. I doubted she read books—she never stopped to browse or even look at the gifts or magazines, and had never made a purchase.

"We've got our eye on you," she said menacingly.

I didn't know who "we" were, and I was much too afraid to ask. At one point a small group of seniors had tried to picket my store right after I opened, a few of them holding signs that read things like NO DIRTY STUFF IN OUR TOWN and KEEP BIG CITY PORN AWAY FROM OUR SMALL-TOWN VALUES. One oldster had shown up with a sign that said I LOVE DIRTY BOOKS, but he got yelled at and left shortly thereafter, presumably having been sent home to reassess his priorities.

Leona had been at the helm of the operation, bullhorn in hand. Fortunately, she couldn't figure out how to get it to work, but she did look very imposing while carrying it around.

To break up the protest, I'd had to get Kelly to show up and remind Leona of our agreement regarding the vandalism and break-in. That didn't work, but one quick phone call and five minutes later, a white SUV with the word SHERIFF painted on the side appeared. Everyone vanished in no time flat.

It was a tenuous ceasefire, but it was all I had.

"Everything is fine, Leona, honest. All my books are aboveboard, and everything is running smoothly. Business is pretty good, too. And every time someone compliments me on this beautiful space, I always make a point to tell them it's your building, and that you're a great landlady!" I smiled and held my breath.

It seemed to work. Her expression softened, and this time it looked like she might finally leave the store. I crossed my fingers under the counter.

"Just remember that Guthrie is a good, clean town. We don't need any outsiders coming in with their big city proclivities, making a mess of things."

We stared at each other in silence. What could I say to that? The word *outsider* hurt like a mofo every time she said it, and she said it a lot. All I wanted was to make a good living in my new hometown. I knew it would take a while to be accepted as a local, but she hadn't done much to make me feel welcome. So far she was the biggest hurdle in my new life.

Finally she spoke. "I'm late for a hair appointment." Then she left my store without so much as a backward glance.

I breathed a sigh of relief—it could have been worse, I reasoned. But how many more times would it happen? I'd never convince her that I wasn't a bad person, what with my 'big city proclivities,' as she called them. But I was an Oklahoman just like her, gosh darnit!

I flopped down in one of the comfy reading chairs by the new release tables. One person not warming up to my presence in Guthrie was fine; I could handle that. But what if there were more?

TWO

Monday mornings were usually slow at the Book Store, so it ended up being okay that I was a little bit late opening up. Once I had recovered from Leona's super enjoyable social call, I took care of some light bookkeeping and basic housekeeping activities, like dusting the self-help section. It seemed like the self-help books always got dustier than other sections and I wondered if it was from lack of use, or if it was simply the one place in the store where all the dirt collected. Like an energetic black hole.

It was tough being the owner and only full-time employee; I had to be there almost all the time. Early on I'd hired one part-time employee, Julie. She was a junior over at the high school, and several days a week would cover the shop for the afternoon and come in for a while every other Saturday. But most of the time it was me, on my own with all the books, and sometimes some customers. Hopefully soon I'd be able to give her a few more hours, or even hire another part-timer.

When the self-help books were tidy and dust-free again, it was time to work on my novel. I'd had this brilliant idea when I first opened that I would be able to spend my free time writing my first book. In my previous career, I'd spent so much time working on other people's writing that I hadn't done much of my own. But now I would have the time, and I could finally do it.

That had turned out to be about as naive as thinking it would be easy raising chickens. Lack of time wasn't my problem —I had plenty of free time between customers. The real issue was that I'd discovered I possessed a unique talent, which must have remained dormant up till now, but came to life when I moved to a small town where the pace of life moved slower. I was a master procrastinator. Not amateur level, mind you—I'd become proficient at the professional level. So, not much writing got done. But this was Monday, the first bright shiny day of a new week. I could do this.

I sat down behind the counter and pulled out my novel-outline notepad. The first few pages were filled with doodles and a few notes for character sketches and possible plot lines. I'd decided to write a romance novel, because I loved the idea of a happily ever after ending. Who wouldn't!

I had a few thoughts about what direction I wanted to head, but no concrete ideas and anything resembling a plot outline was nowhere to be found. But today was a new day! My pen was poised over my notepad, ready to put words to paper ... and then I drew some big circles in the middle of the page and started coloring them in. This repetitive motion helped me think, I reasoned.

I looked up from my coloring notepad and noticed a book on the front display table sat ever so slightly askew. Oh dear. I should probably take every book off the table and re-stack them properly. That would keep me busy all the way till lunchtime. No time for novel writing after all. Darn! No one was coming in the door, so no customers either. I began to deconstruct the table.

Just as I placed the last book back on its stack—the book that had caused the whole problem in the first place—my stomach growled, right on cue. Julie walked in the door to start her afternoon shift; she had half-days at school on Mondays and came in to cover my lunch. Thank goodness! Time to head over to Stacy's Place. I filled Julie in on what to do while I was gone, and left.

Every Monday, I met my lawyer and new best friend Kelly Passicheck for lunch at Stacy's, and I usually walked there, checking out the other shops along the way. The breeze was still as brisk as ever, and my hair whipped in front of my face again. I made another mental note that I really needed to invest in a hat because this was ridiculous.

I passed the chocolate shop as the door opened and someone walked out, carrying with them some amazing chocolatey scents. My stomach grumbled its approval. I was definitely ready for lunch.

Guthrie was a picturesque town, about an hour north of the state capital of Oklahoma City. It used to be the capital when Oklahoma was merely a territory. When the territory became a state and grew more populated, Guthrie lost the title of capital to OKC. There were multiple versions of the story behind how it had happened, but my favorite was something about someone climbing in a window to steal the official state seal and taking it to the new capital. Or something equally silly. After the oil boom of the '20s, things went slowly downhill and now many of the storefronts and historical buildings sat empty, while plenty of people continuously complained about how much better the good ol' days were.

But there were signs of new activity, like the yarn shop that featured a colorful window display and offered classes every Saturday (not that I was a knitter; that was old lady stuff, mind you). And my cool new bookstore, of course.

As I passed several antique shops, the owners waved at me through their big front windows, and I waved back, happy for the acknowledgment. Guthrie also housed several galleries, a few restaurants, and even one fantastic coffee shop. Yup, I was hopeful for my bookstore and for the town.

I continued along the block, admiring the tops of the old buildings across the street, with their ornate window trim and fancy brick- and stonework. One building had the year 1904 embedded on a date stone above the entrance. I wondered what the building originally housed way back then. Maybe something that had been modern and fancy at the time, only to be lost in obscurity and now permanently forgotten.

I arrived at Stacy's ten minutes early, as I always did. Fortunately, I took a book to read everywhere I went so I had something to do while I waited. Our regular waitress, Bonnie, had two iced teas already on the table, along with two menus. She was good, and we were predictable.

Stacy's Place was the perfect lunch spot, and Kelly and I weren't the only ones who made it our regular hangout. Anybody who was anyone in Guthrie would meet there for lunch, and you could even check out the tourists (yes, we had tourists), all while having a delicious down-home meal. I had a real soft spot for the chicken salad sandwich, with its mound of mayo-heavy chicken, celery, and grape mixture served between two slices of perfectly toasted sprouted grain bread. Heaven.

Kelly was my attorney and also my best friend. She was the only practicing female attorney in Guthrie, and she owned her own practice. As such, she had a lot of women as clients who were very often quite bitter, because they needed divorces from their husbands who were either cheating, unappreciative, or workaholics, and sometimes all three. In truth she was the go-to attorney for most women in town who needed any kind of legal help. She was unfussy, approachable, hopelessly fair, and always willing to represent the underdog. Which basically meant she was incredibly busy yet still drove an unimpressive car.

When I needed help with the contract for the bookstore, and then with the hullabaloo with Leona, Kelly had proven to be a tenacious and knowledgeable attorney, who then ended up being a good friend with a quick, dry sense of humor. We discovered we had a lot in common, and I was so happy to have a friend like her in my new hometown.

As I looked around the room, I realized several people were glaring at me. They all appeared to be seniors. One lady, whom I recognized from the brief yet memorable picketing incident, pointed the index and middle fingers of one hand first at her own eyes, then turned them around and pointed them at me. Uh-oh. I just hoped she wasn't putting some kind of weird country curse on me. I pulled out my book and pretended to read. I was starving and couldn't wait for Kelly to get there.

After an indeterminate amount of time had passed—it felt like an hour but was probably only a minute or two—I looked up hopefully at the front door in time to see Kelly walk in and spot me at our regular booth. She made her way across the crowded restaurant and slid into the bench seat across from me. Then she dumped a big pile of manila folders onto the side of the table, a slight furrow to her brow. I noticed that each folder had a rubber band around it to keep the contents from spilling out.

"You know they have these things now called briefcases," I said nonchalantly, quickly looking down at my book. She said nothing, but I could almost hear her scowl become deeper. I had made a mistake and momentarily forgot that she abhorred briefcases; it was part of her campaign to be more of a "attorney of the people." I guess you had to be messy to be accessible. In any case, I decided on the spot to buy her a nice book bag for Christmas. It was worth a try.

I tucked my book away. "So what's new?" I hoped that a

quick subject change would unfurrow her brow, although I was doubtful.

"Oh, not much," she answered, taking out her reading glasses. She put them on and started looking over the menu in front of her. "Huge caseload. Corrupt legal system. Women being overpowered and manipulated by the patriarchy. You know, just the usual bullshit."

"Ah." What could I say to that? Go with your gut, Beverley. "So what are you ordering today?"

She glanced at me over the top of her readers and tried to look serious but ended up grinning because I was wiggling my eyebrows at her in anticipation of her answer. She exhaled heavily and closed the menu, taking her glasses back off. "Oh, I guess I'll have my usual."

I waved at Bonnie and gave her a quick signal indicating we would both be having our usual. The signal consisted of me pointing at Kelly, then at myself, and ending with a shrug. Bonnie nodded and walked to the kitchen to put in our orders: one chicken salad sandwich and one fried chicken plate. It was a true wonder of the universe that Kelly was as healthy as she was, considering the way she ate.

"What's new with you?" she asked me. She glanced at her phone but apparently didn't find anything of interest on it, because she immediately tossed it onto the stack of folders and leaned back into the bench seat.

"The chickens got out again this morning," I answered in a sheepish voice. Or maybe that was chickenish.

"I told you not to get chickens, Beverley," she admonished. She had that tone in her voice. You know the one. People like to use it when you admit to a mistake they knew you were going to make all along.

"Bah!" I waved my hand at her with an air of carelessness. "They're great. Pretty soon they'll calm down, and then you'll see. I'll be selling eggs as well as books." So far they hadn't even produced enough for me to enjoy an occasional omelet, but I knew it was only a matter of time. They just didn't feel at home yet. We hadn't quite fully bonded. It was all Beryl's fault.

"Okay then, good luck with that." Kelly shrugged, and I could tell she was dropping the subject but was also clearly taking great pleasure in being proven right in her belief that chickens were no darned good—except if they were fried, put on a dinner plate, and served with some mashed potatoes and gravy.

We made some small talk about the weather, Kelly's never-ending caseload, and the nonexistent outline for my nonexistent novel. I asked how her husband, Ben, was doing, and she answered, as she usually did, that he was fine and "still along for the ride."

As I was about to faint from hunger, Bonnie appeared with two gigantic plates of food and set them down in front of us. Kelly's fried chicken smelled delicious, but I could also feel my arteries clogging as I inhaled. We started eating and fell silent for a while. As our face-stuffing pace slowed, the conversation picked up again and Kelly asked about my store, and which books were selling the best. The Book Store had both fiction and nonfiction titles, and depending on what was popular at any given time, both sold well. Except for self-help, go figure. Overall, Guthrie seemed to be a fiction kind of town. Women's fiction sold decently, as did crime fiction and mysteries.

"What's women's fiction exactly?" she asked as she worked through her obligatory scoop of green beans.

"Oh, you know, books with female lead characters, written for women. It's kind of a vague heading, really. There are all kinds of subgenres that fall under women's fiction." I could feel myself getting animated as I started talking about books. I could spend a lot of time doing that.

"What's a subgenre?" she asked, looking at me. She never minded humoring me, bless her heart.

"You're kidding, right?" I pointed my fork at her, then remembered that this was probably impolite. I pointed it toward the ceiling instead and silently thanked her for asking me more questions about books.

"Yes. But seriously, what kinds of things fall under women's fiction? It does seem sort of broad, pardon the pun."

I snorted. "Let's see, romance, chick lit, erotica, to name a few. Then there are subgenres under romance—contemporary, historical, Regency, paranormal, time travel ... I could go on, but I want to finish my sandwich." I knew a lot about women's fiction in particular; it's what I had specialized in when I'd worked in publishing.

"Do you carry all those in your store?"

"No," I answered. "I don't have enough space. I try to sell a little bit of everything, but I'm still trying to figure out what's most popular."

Kelly hunkered down in her seat and lowered her voice. "So has anyone come in asking for any, you know, weird stuff?"

I almost spit out my iced tea at her as I stifled a laugh. "Maybe," I said just as quietly. "But that is covered by bookseller–reader confidentiality." I took another bite of my delicious sandwich. "It also depends on what you consider weird. But for kicks, go ahead and do an internet search on dinosaur erotica later and see what comes up."

This time it was Kelly who almost sprayed iced tea across the table. "Uh, okay..."

We sat in silence for a few more bites, Kelly looking thoughtful. "What about Bigfoot?" she asked.

"Say what now?" I peered at her over the last half of my sandwich.

"Is there Bigfoot erotica?" She wiped the grease off her fingers and looked around the booth, probably searching for more fried chicken.

My sandwich fell out of my hand and landed back on my

plate. A grape fell out of it, rolling across the table and onto the floor.

"Excuse me?" I said, wide-eyed.

Kelly sighed, like I was the biggest idiot ever. "Dirty books about Bigfoot. I'd think that would be self-explanatory."

"I guess," I said slowly. "I suppose could do a search on that and let you know." I knew as I said it I had no actual plans to do it.

"You should! I think it would sell well here." She sat back and crossed her arms, watching me. "We have them around here, you know. Have you seen one yet?"

"Wait. You're asking me if I've seen an erotic Bigfoot?" I couldn't comprehend what she was getting at. My mind kept trying to translate this line of conversation into a more benign subject, like shoe shopping or flower arranging.

"No, just a regular Bigfoot. Um, to be honest, I don't know how erotic they are. But—oh lord, this is getting weird."

"Really?" I smirked.

"We do have Sasquatches around here. I thought you knew that. Haven't you had a sighting yet?"

"What exactly do you mean by 'sighting'?" My brain was still not connecting all the dots. They were weird, scary dots.

Kelly sighed again, this time with a dramatic drop of her shoulders that indicated she was losing patience with me, and fast.

"Seriously, what the heck kind of question is that? 'Haven't you had a sighting yet?'" I tried to sound like I was mocking her, but I could feel my palms getting clammy and a slight sweat breaking out on my forehead. "Do they buy a lot of books or something? Is there a Sasquatch trailer park nearby? Why on earth would I see a Bigfoot?" This topic was new territory for me. It was as if someone had suddenly thrown down a speed bump in the middle of a parking lot that I usually took at forty miles per hour. My teeth slammed together, and I started to worry about what might have happened to my suspension.

Kelly scooped up the last of her mashed potatoes and dredged them through her cup of extra gravy. "Dinosaur, Bigfoot, it wasn't that big of a stretch. You're bound to see one eventually. It's just a matter of time before everyone around here calls in a Bigfoot sighting."

"To whom, the Justice League of America?"

"No, to the sheriff. Hey, I'm serious! It's a thing, you know. It's gonna happen."

I leaned back and laughed. "Yeah, I don't think so. Not to this Guthrie resident."

"Uh-huh," Kelly said with that tone. The one that was waiting to prove me wrong. Only I wasn't going to let her.

"Have *you* seen one?"

"Yup!" she said proudly, sitting up straight. Then she slouched. "Sort of. Maybe."

I wasn't letting her off easy, mostly because it was such blatant bullpoop. "You either have or you haven't, Kelly. Like inhaling. Or sex."

She looked confused for a minute, but finally gave up trying to form an argument. "Okay, fine, I've never seen one myself. But I've talked to lots of people who have. People you wouldn't think believe in Bigfoot. So the evidence is compelling."

I was surprised by this. Kelly was a logical, rational woman. "Come on, that's ridiculous. I don't believe you. There's no such thing! Sasquatch is a hoax; it's been disproved like a billion different times."

She raised an eyebrow at me.

"Oh please!" I was getting agitated, but I wasn't exactly sure why. Maybe because the conversation was so incredibly pointless. "Anyone who believes in that hooey is certifiably crazy. Or plain stupid."

"You may want to rethink that, Bev," she said, leaning

forward and reaching for the check. "If we had to commit everyone in town who believed in Bigfoot, no one would be left. And I happen to have a very high IQ, thank you very much. I'm telling you—you will see him. Or her. Or whatever. Your house is a little farther outside of town, and a lot of sightings happen out that way."

I was speechless. But only for a few seconds because then the questions came fast and furious. I started bouncing my left leg around under the table as a way to vent my mounting anxiety. A rivulet of sweat trickled down my back. "How on earth do you know where most Bigfoot sightings occur in Guthrie? And why on earth do you care?"

"I don't know. Call it a hobby, I guess." She was making me nervous, and I could tell she was loving it. "Why, are you scared of Bigfoot, Bev?" Her eyebrows rose.

As a reply to her question, I thought about running out of the restaurant screaming in terror and heading in the general direction of Texas. Instead, I resisted the urge to flee the state and kept sitting in my seat. "Nah," I said in a voice that wouldn't have fooled a five-year-old. "I just think they're dumb." I grabbed my napkin and wiped my forehead.

"Relax," she said in a halfway decent attempt at a soothing voice. "I mean, it's not like one has ever killed anyone. That we know of, anyway." My leg stopped bouncing. A small smile showed at the corner of her mouth as she picked up her phone to check the time. "Oh shit, I've got to run. I'll catch up with you later," she said as she tossed some money on the table, picked up all her files, and left the restaurant, leaving me sitting there wondering what had just happened.

Bigfoot? In my backyard? Yeah, not so much.

After settling the bill, I said goodbye to Bonnie and left the restaurant. I stood outside for a minute, still considering making a run for Texas. I tried to get the image of a big hairy monster killing people out of my head. The idea that Bigfoot might exist terrified me. Like, a level-ten type of terrified. The kind of terrified that sends people into therapy for years. I took three deep breaths and started walking. There was no way that they could be real. No way. I didn't care what my best friend said. She could be the best feminist lawyer in the world, but she was dead wrong on this topic.

As I walked back to the shop I noticed the shadows had gotten a little longer during my lunch break, and an almost imperceptible change in the weather had occurred. Somehow the air was a little different—maybe a little less humid, or the breeze now came from a slightly different direction. Whatever it was, it signaled that a transition to a new season was close at hand, and it felt pretty good. But as I kept walking, it seemed like the shift in the air was signaling some other kind of event. Something more mysterious. Or scary. I couldn't quite put my finger on it. Maybe it was all the Bigfoot talk. Or maybe it was simply that I hadn't been back in Oklahoma long enough to be familiar with all the subtle seasonal changes. Yeah, that was probably it.

THREE

Every Monday afternoon I took an extra-long lunch so I could attend the staff meeting for the Guthrie *Ledger,* the local paper. Because in addition to raising chickens, running the Book Store, and settling into my new town, I had decided to also find a part-time job. The paper's editor, Mark Ellison, insisted that everyone show up each Monday, right after lunchtime. I tried to ask him once if we could move the meetings to Monday morning, or maybe later in the afternoon. But nope, he wanted them Mondays after lunch.

One Monday a few months earlier, I was running late for my lunch with Kelly, and I texted her, asking if she could order for me. When I got there, Molly brought me a double cheeseburger and onion rings and I ended up falling asleep in that afternoon's *Ledger* meeting. As payback, Mark made me write an article about new sanitation practices at the city dump. I also had to go take pictures and interview the CEO and hadn't been able to object because I'd been napping in the corner. That was the week I started bringing coffee to the meetings, and that was also the last time I ever let Kelly order for me.

Cappuccinos were my secret weapon against involuntary

napping during *Ledger* meetings, and thank the stars above I'd discovered a place within walking distance where I could get a great cuppa joe. It turned out it was also the only cafe where I could get *real* coffee in Guthrie. Hoboken Coffee Roasters was housed in an old metal-walled garage, set back from Division Street. You pretty much had to be in the know; the only indication that the best coffee within a fifty-mile radius was right under your nose was a small sandwich board sign out on the sidewalk directing you to the hidden promised land tucked behind an abandoned gas station.

As I started out on my walk, I had a strange feeling that I was being watched. The conversation with Kelly about Bigfoot had spooked me plenty, so I tried to chalk it up to simple paranoia. I did my best to shake it off, but that little irksome sensation kept coming back.

I got to Division Street and had to wait for the light to turn green before crossing. As I stood watching the cars go by, something made me swivel my head to the left, and I caught a glimpse of someone ducking behind a corner. It was a flash of white hair—it had been there and then it was gone. Sasquatches weren't white, were they? No, those were abominable snowmen, if I was remembering my scary fictional cryptids correctly. So it had to have been a person. Whether or not they were really following me was another question.

It was my turn to cross, so I walked to the other side of the street and continued toward the coffee shop. Still not able to shake that weird feeling, I stopped abruptly and spun around. Sure enough, there was someone behind me. He was a short, rotund man with wispy white hair, and by the way he carried himself I guessed him to be at least in his sixties. His eyes were hidden by a pair of what looked an awful lot like women's sunglasses, and he wore a black button-down shirt with polyester plaid pants that were almost as wide as they were long.

As soon as he noticed I'd turned around, he looked to his left and then his right, as if searching for an escape route. To his right was oncoming traffic, to his left was the huge window of a travel agency storefront. His choices seemed to be slim. I narrowed my eyes as I watched to see what he would do next. He was starting to look panicked, poor fella.

I was about to say something, but he turned around and ran away from me until he disappeared around a corner. Definitely not Bigfoot; probably one of those bookstore picketers trying to hassle me again. At least I hoped so, otherwise he was a plain old creepy guy. If I'd wanted to be followed by those, I'd have stayed in New York. I shook my head, turned, and went on to the coffee shop.

I had no idea why the owners of Hoboken had named a coffee shop in Oklahoma after a city in New Jersey. Someday I'd have to write an article about them and find out all the background, but for today it would remain a mystery.

The place was almost always packed. Today every available chair was occupied by people drinking coffee or tea, while they visited with friends or worked alone on their laptops. A coffee shop like Hoboken was hipster through and through, with its austere decor, concrete countertops, and working turntable paired with a shelf full of vinyl records. No CDs or music streaming in this joint.

Hoboken was also a classic example of new school meets old school. At least half the patrons wore skinny jeans and sported earbuds. But the place also appealed to GenXers like me. We were older and thoroughly jaded, yet we were still tech-savvy enough to need a place to get caffeinated while looking for new jobs on our laptops. And there were even old-timers sprinkled into the crowd, drinking black coffee and watching their grandkids eat vegan raspberry crumble muffins.

I loved coming to Hoboken and taking the pulse of my new city. Coffee brought everyone together, and always made everything better. The day I discovered this place, I almost cried with joy. I hadn't been sure I'd be able to live in a town without a decent place for a cappuccino. And now I'd never have to find out.

As I waited for Seth, owner and also my favorite barista, to make my cappuccino, I watched a man walk in the door. I hadn't seen him around before, and I wondered if this was because he wasn't a local, or if his timing had simply been bad up till now.

I looked him over. Leisurely. I gazed upon him like he was a porcelain six-ounce cappuccino cup filled to the brim with espresso and smooth, sweet steamed milk. With a chocolate almond biscotti on the side. I told myself it was okay to think these thoughts. No one seemed to notice my ogling, and no one else in the whole wide world had to know I was comparing a man to a cappuccino and a cookie. I also reasoned that I didn't always want to be staring at my phone; it was rude.

He was extremely good-looking. I was always on the lookout for the elusive Really Good-Looking Man, and considered myself a connoisseur, having years of practical observation. But these days, the RGLM seemed harder to find. On the rare occasion I did see one, my interest was immediately piqued. Like today.

Either I was getting pickier as I got older, or most men weren't aging well. In which case, my choices for potential romantic partners were dwindling fast, minute by minute. But if they weren't aging well, maybe I wasn't aging all that great either. And lord only knew what they thought about me. An existential panic began to set in, and I started to think maybe I was screwed.

I tried to shake the mounting sense of having lost something I'd never had to begin with. Maybe I could convince my brain to shut up and go back to the simple pleasure of ogling. I could admire this good-looking person and leave it at that. *Zip it, brain!*

The Really Good-Looking Man had walked farther into the shop and now stood in line to order. And I kept on stealth-ogling. Sometimes a man who was that handsome would, upon closer inspection, turn out to be a jerk, or act as if he were too awesome for his own good. But I could already tell this guy was different. He looked friendly and approachable, with a calm, easy presence.

He wasn't very tall, maybe five foot nine or ten, but he had a lean, defined figure. His hair was sandy blond and curly, and it looked a little windblown, like he'd been outside a while. His bright blue eyes lit up the shop as he smiled and nodded to Seth. It made me smile a little, too. I forgot that I was trying to scope him out on the down-low. I caught myself and looked away, hoping no one had noticed.

But before too long, my gaze slowly moved back to him. I wished I could see his hands, but they were tucked into the pockets of his jeans. I liked to think I could tell a lot about a man by his hands. And his shoes—they also spoke volumes about his character. It had nothing to do with size; it was about quality. I'd always been a "quality over quantity" advocate.

Naturally, my gaze traveled south toward his feet (noting briefly along the way how nicely his jeans fit) and landed on a pair of expensive boots. Expensive, but worn. Quality over quantity. Either I had discovered a previously undiagnosed heart murmur, or he was making my chest a little fluttery.

When he finally got to the counter, he greeted Seth like they were old friends, and ordered a cappuccino. Huh. He was good-looking and he had good taste in coffee. An appealing combination. Yup, nice boots, cute dude. Which morphed into the name Mr. Cute Boots. I knew that was a stupid name, but it was the first thing that popped into my mind, so I went with it for now and made plans to admonish myself later.

Suddenly I heard Seth calling my name in a way that sounded like it might be the third or fourth time he'd said it. The handsome stranger looked my way, and I could feel my cheeks getting red. Drat! I was too old for this blushing baloney, but it still happened anyway.

To get my cappuccino, I had to walk up next to him. How to play this? With not much time to decide, I went for the opposite of my usual New York aloof persona. I gathered my five feet and five inches up as tall as I could and looked him in the eye as I approached the counter. I gave him a hint of a smile as I picked up my paper to-go cup, thanked Seth, turned to leave, and promptly dropped my phone. It fell right out of my hand and landed with a very loud *slap!* on the concrete floor. Right at Mr. Cute Boots' boots.

Oh dear. Now I was flustered. I bent down to pick up my phone and was halfway there when it occurred to me that oh, this might be getting too far up into Mr. Cute Boots' personal space. So I stopped, mid-bend. Then I proceeded to spill my coffee. On my phone. And maybe on his boots. I was too discombobulated to check all that closely.

I was now frozen, mid-stoop, and in grave danger of completely losing my cool. I started to panic. Did I continue to reach down and pick up my phone? Should I stand back up and run out of the shop with half a cappuccino and no phone? Maybe I should just faint.

Before I could do anything, Mr. Cute Boots pulled some napkins from a stack on the counter and bent down to pick up my phone. Then he stood up and wiped it off. I stood up too, and he extended his hand, my phone resting on a napkin on his palm. All nice and clean. I still had enough of my wits about me to be disappointed I couldn't see his hand underneath the napkin.

"Here you go," he said in a very smooth voice.

I was blushing even more by then. As I reached out to take my phone, I did manage to look directly at him, and was able to get a better look at his clear blue eyes. They were the shade of blue that zapped you right down to your bones and in the process read every single thought in your brain, especially the dirty ones. I'd never seen anything like it in person before, but I'd read about eyes like those. In romance novels.

I took my phone from his outstretched palm and almost spilled the rest of my coffee. Could this get any worse? Probably.

"Thank you," I replied as coolly as I could. However, it was possible my voice wasn't working properly, and I may have said "Fruit moose" instead. Oh my god. I was acting like a befuddled thirteen-year-old. I hoped I hadn't said *that* part out loud. I stuffed my phone in the back pocket of my jeans. If my face got any hotter someone would need to call the fire department.

He glanced at the cup in my hand. "Would you like another cappuccino? You could take mine." He held his own drink out to me. By this point, I could no longer look him in the eye. It was like I was scared? Oh my gosh, that was it. I was now scared. I heard his voice say the words, and all I could do was pretend to search for my keys. Which didn't take long because I didn't have a purse or bag, and they were dangling from the front pocket of my jeans.

"Um, no thanks, I'm good. But thanks." I managed another quick peek at his face. His eyes were laughing. Were they laughing *at* me? Or *with* me? I wasn't laughing. That meant he couldn't be laughing with me. So therefore he was laughing at me. And why wouldn't he? Here I was, a full-grown woman, acting like a giant dork. Expressly for the purpose of Mr. Cute Boots' amusement.

"Okay then." He turned back to the counter and continued talking to Seth. I headed for the door as quickly as I could.

I stopped at the back of the shop to grab some napkins, because this episode didn't bode well for me walking safely all the way to the *Ledger* offices, even if the cup was only half-full at this point. I pulled a few napkins out of the dispenser and heard Seth and the stranger laugh. I looked back at them, and they were both watching me. Mr. Cute Boots' eyes were so freakin' sparkly, I could hardly stand it. Oh, sweet baby James, I was about to have a meltdown right then and there. I wondered if there was any way I could salvage any of my dignity. I sighed. Probably not. So why not go out in style?

I took a deep breath, flipped my brown shoulder-length curls, and sauntered out the door with what I hoped was a walk that looked good from behind. Because why the heck not.

FOUR

I had been so flustered by the coffee incident that I forgot to check if I was being followed until I was almost in front of the *Ledger* offices. I arrived only a few minutes late, and I took a quick look up and down the street before opening the front door: no old dude in women's sunglasses anywhere. That I saw, anyway. I shrugged, went inside, and headed for the conference room.

I'd taken the gig with the *Ledger* not long after I'd moved to town. Even though I'd never been a reporter before, Mark Ellison had been so excited to have a big-time New York book nerd on his staff that he'd hired me before I'd even come in to visit the office. It hadn't hurt that we'd gone to school together in OKC, and that he'd had a huge crush on me in eighth grade. But those crushes fade as quickly as ice cream melts on the summer sunbaked sidewalk, and we'd lost touch after high school—he'd gone to Kansas University to study journalism, and I'd gone off to New York. When I started doing research on Guthrie, I checked out the *Ledger* masthead and discovered he had settled in my new hometown. It turned out he'd taken a job here right out of college and had been with the paper ever since. He probably wanted to be near—but not too close—to his parents, just like me. Smart guy.

The best part about working at the paper wasn't the infinitesimal salary, but rather the social aspect of the job. Writing for the *Ledger* was a great way to meet people all over town. I got to know what kind of businesses people had, and what kinds of things were important to people. It helped me understand and appreciate my new hometown more. And every time I went out on an assignment, it was an opportunity for me to introduce myself and let people get to know me.

It also turned out that I loved writing news articles. I'd had one or two journalism classes in college but hadn't done any nonfiction writing since then, save for editorial comments and such. Now that I was at the *Ledger,* I could hone my skills. It was a nice complement to writing fiction, or at least it would be —if I were writing any fiction.

By the time I made it to the conference room I'd come up with a fake excuse for my tardiness. Something about having to give a witness statement to the police about A Very Important Thing. But it turned out an excuse wasn't necessary, because Mark hadn't made it in yet.

A few other employees were already there (not that there were many of us to begin with), and Grace, the assistant editor, was sitting at the head of the table. All of us knew—including Grace—that she would have to switch seats when Mark got there, but she liked to imagine she was the boss. So we all let her. There didn't seem to be any harm in it.

Grace once mentioned she believed in the Law of Attraction. I didn't know much about it myself, but I thought it had something to do with the premise of *like attracts like*. It seemed that Grace might have a flawed understanding of the basic principles, though. She liked to imagine she already had what she wanted. Hey, whatever floated her boat, I figured. But then she would complain when whatever she was pretending to have didn't show up in real life. She would always talk about her "boyfriend" when we all knew she didn't have one, and wasn't likely to attract one if she kept cavorting around town holding hands with an imaginary man, no matter how handsome he was purported to be. But to paraphrase one of my favorite aphorisms, to each her own imaginary boyfriend.

As soon as I parked myself in a chair and took on an air of being bored from having been there for ages, Mark entered the room in his usual huff. Suddenly everyone was sitting up a little taller, with their pencils poised at the ready over their notebooks. He looked at Grace sitting in his chair, and she sighed forlornly before scooting over one seat. Mark strode across the room, and I admired him as he did so. He'd been attractive way back when, and now he was one of those men who was aging well. His espresso-brown hair had a few flecks of gray in it, and it suited him. His dark eyes were often guarded but alluring. Almost sultry.

Ack! I needed to snap out of it. I took a big sip from my to-go cup as a preemptive strike against napping.

"Sorry I'm late, guys," Mark said as he sat down heavily in his chair. "The ad department seems to have their heads stuck up their collective ass again." He carelessly tossed a stack of papers onto the table, and they slid all over the place. This was his way of passing out copies to everyone. He wasn't known for being much of a hand-holder, or even for being very pleasant, for that matter. Apparently manners and a congenial personality didn't get you very far in the newspaper business. Which was the polar opposite of the publishing business. I made a split-second decision to never go into newspaper editing.

It also seemed that a long, contentious divorce could wreak havoc on your ability to be happy, or even just plain nice to people. Poor guy. Still, he was old enough to know better. But he was the boss, so the rest of us would have to deal with it.

"John, what's the deal on the article about the latest usage proposal for the State Capital Company Building?" And with that, Mark started his no-fuss, no-muss rundown of outstanding articles. Once he had grilled everyone about their current assignments, he started handing out new ones. Jade got a story about the new candle shop opening at the corner of Oklahoma and Broad, Grace was assigned to the next meeting of the Guthrie Quilting Guild, and Burns got a story about hard times that had befallen a local chicken farmer. Dang, some people had all the luck. I wondered if I had been left out of the next round, but then Mark turned to me.

"Beverley, Al Turner phoned in a Bigfoot sighting to the sheriff's office yesterday. It's the second call in a week. I want you to go talk to Al. And get with Leona Tisdale too. She says one was rooting through her trash last Friday. It's been a while since we've run a Bigfoot story, so go ahead and put together a comprehensive piece."

"Wait, did you just say 'Bigfoot'?" I asked, trying to sound casual but realizing it may have come out sounding more panic-stricken than carefree. I hoped my eyes didn't have that spirally, crazy look they sometimes got when I was anxious. "You mean, like, Sasquatch Bigfoot?"

Mark exhaled a forceful breath and threw his pencil on the table. "What other Bigfoot is there, Bev? You fancy New Yorkers got something fancier up East?" This last remark elicited a smirk from several of my fellow employees, who hadn't exactly warmed up to the idea of having one of those fancy New Yorkers in their midst yet, even if she was originally an Okie. And questioning the existence of Bigfoot, right after my boss assigned me what was supposed to be an investigative article about them, might not be the way to go very far toward ditching my outsider status. I was still at square one with these people, and Mark knew how to push my buttons. Even so, I couldn't help myself.

"It's the same Bigfoot up East too, presumably," I began, trying to sound knowledgeable. "The same imaginary, fake Bigfoot."

Mark pointed his finger at me in protest and opened his mouth to speak, but I cut him off.

"Mark! Everyone knows that Bigfoot isn't real. You really want me to write a serious news story on a fictional character?" I laughed like this was the most preposterous idea ever—because it was. I sputtered and scoffed, "Nobody is going to go for something like that."

"Beverley!" he shot back at me. "Everyone will go for something like that. Bigfoot is not fictional. Go get me a story. A real story. Show us small-town folks how it's done, why don't you."

Clearly the crush he had on me in eighth grade was no longer winning me any additional brownie points. He rose from his chair and scooped up his stack of papers and his pencil, which had landed on the other side of the table when he'd thrown it. Then he stalked out the door, leaving me with no choice but to look each remaining person in the eye one by one, trying to confirm that I was truly expected to go write a news story about a made-up monster.

But no one met my pleading, crazy-person gaze. They all looked down at their notepads and wrote very important pretend notes. Then they all shuffled out of the room one by one, without so much as a conciliatory, "Good luck with that, Bev."

I sat in the conference room by myself for a few minutes, unable to move. I felt like I was an alien from the Rational Galaxy who had crash landed on Planet What the Heck. I started to get that clammy, anxious feeling again. I took a few deep breaths, got up from my chair, and walked straight to Mark's office, where he had barricaded himself behind the two giant computer monitors placed strategically in the middle of his desk. All I could see was the top of his head over the screens, part of a keyboard on the surface of the desk, and his coffee cup next to the keyboard. The pencil was MIA. I gently closed the door behind me. This situation called for an approach other than logic.

"Maaark." I lengthened and smoothed out his name to make it sound like sweet maple syrup, like we were the best buddies in the whole world. Maybe I could sweet-talk my way out of this pretend article and into a real assignment, like the one about the chicken farmer. "You're not serious about the whole Sasquatch thing, right?" I smiled, hoping he would peer around his computer screens to notice I was batting my eyelashes at him.

But he didn't look up. "Yup, I'm serious." A hint of anger crept into his voice. Then came the sound of the pencil being slammed firmly on the surface of the desk. I knew it was his pencil because I could practically hear the lead breaking in its wooden casing. Poor pencil.

Mark leaned his head around the side of his barricade of monitors and gave me a look that singed my once-fluttering eyelashes. Maybe this hadn't been such a good idea after all. He stood up now, rising to his full six feet and putting his hands on his hips in a defensive posture. "Look, just go write it, okay? What's the big deal? You haven't had a problem with any of your other assignments."

"Yeah, but you've always given me actual news stories to write. This isn't news, it's..."

"Of course it's news. At least, to people around here it is. We do things differently in Guthrie. We're not like you uppity urban New York hipsters. If a few people saw Bigfoot over the weekend, then it's a story. End of story."

"First off, this is not real news!"

"And?"

"And I am not an urban hipster!" I snapped. "If you'd do your research, you'd know that the age demographic for the cultural term hipster—"

This time it was his turn to cut me off.

"If it's not news, then what in god's name is it?" He was getting thoroughly mad at me. I watched for steam to start coming out of his ears.

"—but there is some disagreement as to the exact start date of the age group coined the Millennial generation—"

"For chrissake, Bev," Mark said quietly. Uh-oh.

Instead of running away very fast like I should have, I spewed the truth all over his desk instead. "Okay, it isn't actual news. It's science fiction. It's ridiculous, is what it is."

"Beverley. Stop arguing and go write the blasted story already."

"Yeah, but..." My voice trailed off.

"But what? I don't have time for this. What? What is it already?" He was pleading with me now so he could get me out of his office once and for all.

"Couldn't I trade stories with someone?" I tried the maple syrup approach again. "You could give my story to someone who, um, has more experience with Bigfoot."

Mark walked around his desk and placed his hand on my shoulder. My skin grew a little warmer, and I relaxed a little bit until I realized that he was using the maple syrup approach on me now. He shoved me out the door of his office which he had opened without me noticing.

"I think you're the perfect man for the job, Green," he said with one final push to my shoulder. "Go get 'em." I stumbled across the threshold and heard the door slam shut behind me before I could turn around and ask him what the heck I was supposed to go get exactly, and before I could yell at him for calling me a man. I was pretty sure he knew I wasn't actually a man. Right? So what had he meant by that?

Oh. I got it then. He wanted me to grow a pair. What a tool! No wonder his ex-wife divorced him. I made a mental note to let the air out of his tires on my way back to my shop. So much for the syrup approach. That rat bastard.

FIVE

Back at the bookstore, I sat behind the counter and waited for the crowds to roll in. And by crowds, that meant Myrna and Justin Miller, who came in every Monday to pick out one new book each. He would buy a western or a US history book; she would usually get a romance novel. But today they were late. Not that I was paying attention that closely or anything.

I knew from the start it would take time for my shop to get established and for sales to pick up. My rational, business mind knew I would have to work hard at gaining people's trust and friendship, and until that happened, I needed to be patient. Things would be slow and I'd need to sit tight, and eventually, sales would increase. I had accounted for all this when I'd created my budget for the bookstore, but that didn't keep me from getting antsy sometimes when my cash register went too long without seeing any action. Personally, I could go long periods of time without seeing any action, but I kinda wanted my cash register to get some.

Julie had gone to to the library so she could study for a test. I sat in the quiet, empty shop and asked myself once again why I had moved here. No answer came through the door. I took a deep breath and reminded myself once again to be patient. After all, I could always spend my time working on my Bigfoot article. I could even write an entire series of articles about the various cryptids of the world. Starting with Sasquatch!

I felt a knot form in my stomach. This article was getting to me. I hadn't wanted to admit to myself why this was, but there was no denying it any longer. I was plain scared of Bigfoot—had been ever since I was seven. Some people had a fear of getting stuck in an elevator, or of being buried alive, or of being eaten by a giant moth. My biggest concern in life was being captured by Bigfoot and held hostage, forced to clean his cave and make him dinner. As I got older my fears morphed to include other ungodly and unmentionable acts, like having to trim his ear hair or wash his beastly undergarments. If I'd wanted any of that, I'd be married. Which might explain why I wasn't currently married.

It was all my family's fault, god bless them. For my seventh birthday party, my parents had thought it would be great fun to hire someone dressed in a girl Bigfoot costume to visit and play games with the kids. My friends and I were sitting at a little kid table, wearing birthday hats and eating snacks, when Miss Squatch jumped out from behind a tree and scared the living daylights out of us. I think it was me who started screaming my head off first, and then my friends joined in. We were inconsolable and uncontrollable, running around bawling and not watching where we were going. In the mayhem, my friend Joey broke his arm and I ran into the gas grill—you can still see the scar above my left eye.

After Joey left for the doctor and I got my head bandaged, all the parents finally convinced us to meet Miss Squatch again. This time she didn't jump out from behind anything, instead, bringing my birthday cake. It was a tenuous cease-fire, and we were lucky Joey's parents hadn't sued, to be honest.

I couldn't sleep for days, it felt like, and I started having nightmares. I'd insist on sleeping with my parents. And even though my little sister Emily was only five, she thought it was all terribly funny every time we sat down to dinner and I became terrified Miss Squatch was going to pop out of the kitchen and attack us. To this day, I can't see a birthday cake (especially the ones with the big glops of icing flowers) without feeling a little anxious. That doesn't mean I won't eat it—I'm apprehensive, but I'm not crazy.

I eventually got over it enough to live a happy, normal life, and didn't have to tell anybody about my biggest fear. Sometimes I still dreamt about Bigfoot and being kept as his domestic help, but I'd come to think maybe that had more to do with my fear of commitment than Sasquatch himself. And sometimes Emily still brought up the birthday incident, but I love her anyway. Yup, Bigfoot had remained a relatively distant abstract concept, until now.

Sitting behind the counter thinking about Bigfoot gave me a big old case of the heebie-jeebies, and I'd just as soon go back to *not* thinking about it. But here I was, forced to write an article about it, and interview people who believed my biggest irrational fear existed. I would have to do research about a scary monster. I felt light-headed, so I rested my forehead on my hands on the counter.

"Hello, Beverley," I heard a voice say. I looked up to see a petite woman standing right in front of me. I'd been so lost in thought that I hadn't noticed Myrna and Justin had come in to browse.

"Oh hi, Myrna, how's things?"

"Pretty good, pretty good!" she chirped. She was a small woman with delicate features and a long, curved nose. She smiled a lot, and when she spoke, it sounded like she was chirping. I always expected her to take flight every time she left the store. "Say," she went on, "could you help me pick out a book for my grandson this week? He loves tractors."

"I would love to!" I said, springing up from my stool. I was glad for the business and the distraction.

I helped Myrna and Justin find some books, and as they came up to the register to pay, I decided to take their pulse on the whole Bigfoot thing.

"Hey, Justin, you don't believe in Bigfoot, do you?" I watched his face closely as he listened to my question. I expected him to laugh or look surprised, but he didn't even bat an eye. He did pause though, and as I waited for him to answer I tried to anticipate what he would say. Something like, *Oh heck no! Bigfoot is stupid and fake, everybody knows that.*

But nope.

"Oh yes," he finally said, running his fingers through his mousy-brown hair. "Absolutely."

Hmm. "Have you, uh, ever seen one?"

"No, I've never seen one, but my dad saw one, way back in the day, and my granddad used to tell all kinds of stories about Bigfoot encounters." Myrna stood by him, nodding emphatically.

Until today, I had taken them for rational people. My mistake. But as long as they kept buying books, I didn't necessarily have to think they were sane.

"I see," I said, trying to sound thoughtful. "Interesting."

"Why do you ask?" Justin said in a squeaky voice. "Have you seen one?" Myrna perked up at that and watched me expectantly.

"No, of course not!" I declared.

"Oh," said Myrna, sounding very disappointed. Her shoulders drooped slightly.

They both looked hurt by my response, and I suddenly felt bad.

"I'm writing an article on Bigfoot for the paper," I explained. "Just trying to do some, what would you call it..." I waved my hand in the air as I reached for the right words. Myth busting? Refuting? "Research."

"You believe in Bigfoot, don't you?" Justin asked, cocking his head at me.

How could I answer that without answering? Normally I'd shout, *Oh heavens no!* but I wanted to keep the Millers as customers. It was a fine line to walk in a small town—you had to leave room for all points of view, but everything you did or said ended up under a microscope. I was starting to think that believing in Bigfoot was up there with topics like religion and politics in Guthrie.

"I'm looking into it," was all I said, smiling broadly. "Maybe I can contact you if I need any good stories?"

"Absolutely!" Justin volunteered.

I thanked him and told him I would let him know if I needed to go back as far as whenever "the day" was for my research. They paid for their books and said some very cheery, chirpy goodbyes before leaving the shop.

I was sad to see them go as they closed the door behind them. I needed another distraction, right away. Reminiscing about my childhood and the origins of my Sasquatch fear was bumming me out.

So I decided to make myself useful and unpack a few boxes that the UPS guy had brought the morning before. He had gotten to my shop before I had and left a stack of packages by the front door. I made a mental note to ask him, once more, to please not leave boxes outside my shop when I wasn't there. There was virtually no crime in the area, but I was still paranoid. When I lived in New York, I learned right quick that you couldn't leave so much as a used plastic fork unattended for twenty seconds without it getting nicked. Being overly cautious and yes, perhaps a bit overly suspicious, had been a habit of mine for over twenty years, and it was a hard habit to break. Also, with a landlady who wasn't above vandalizing her own property, I didn't think it was a good idea to leave my porn stash —I mean books—unattended outside.

Sadly, putting away books didn't work as a diversionary tactic. While I did get a lot of stuff unpacked, I still felt put out about the dumb newspaper assignment. I had trouble focusing on anything longer than ten seconds so I reached for my novel-writing notebook in hopes that might help.

I Married Bigfoot, I scrawled on a fresh page. It could be a romance, or it could be a thriller. Or if this article went south, maybe it could be a true crime or current affairs book! But I couldn't think of anything specific to write about yet, so instead I drew about two hundred little circles all around what little I'd written. This way, the page wouldn't look so empty. I felt better.

Eventually my hand began to cramp up from all the circle drawing, so instead I sat and stared out the front windows of the store, sighing forlornly and often. Nothing about the newspaper article felt right. Even if I didn't have an irrational fear of Bigfoot, that didn't mean writing a serious article about one lurking around Guthrie was in any way rational. These people were crazy if they thought this was normal. It was a ridiculously stupid idea.

"Ha!" I said, proclaiming aloud my superior rational mind. I'd thought I was alone, but then I heard someone with a very gravelly voice clearing their throat somewhere in the back of the store. Oops.

Wait. Who was in the store? I hadn't seen anyone come in. Fear gripped my stomach as my mind immediately conjured up images of Bigfoot browsing in the reference section. It hit me that I wasn't entirely rational either. I was just a different kind of crazy than everyone else.

Eh, it was probably a very nice regular customer back there.

I would go back and check on them ... in a minute. I looked out the window again in time to see a shadowy figure walk slowly past the store. Cue dramatic music

I continued to watch the windows and about fifteen seconds later, the figure slunk by again. This time I caught more detail. They had on a fedora and a black trench coat. Definitely a man. His stature seemed familiar. Something was fishy, but I couldn't put my finger on it.

Time to see who was in the store. I didn't want to sneak up on whoever it was, but at the same time, I wanted to sneak up on whoever it was. I had no idea where they were, so I walked down the aisle closest to the wall until I got to the storage room door at the back of the shop. Then I turned and walked along the back wall. Another noise came from up front, so I headed that way, cutting across the store by weaving through the aisles. I looked at the floor, trying to spot shoes or legs or furry monster feet.

"Oof!" said the gravelly voice as I ran right into its owner. It was a very tall, thin older gentleman.

"Oh gosh, I'm sorry!" I said, backing away quickly. "I was coming to check on you, to see if you needed anything?"

The tall man looked down at me. "Got any beer?"

I tried to gauge how serious he was. Surely he knew what kind of store he was in? From the look on his face, he appeared to be dead serious. "Um, just books," I said.

He shrugged and looked at some of the books on the shelves right in front of us. It was the cooking section. "Got any books on beer?"

"Like, fiction? Or books on how to make beer? Or pictures of beer?"

He paused before answering. "Sure."

"No, sorry."

"Okay." The tall man turned, walked up the aisle, and left the store.

47

I followed close behind until I got to the cash wrap, where I stopped and watched him go. He paused right outside the front door, and the figure in the trench coat walked up to him. They started speaking, but I couldn't make out the words, even though the voices got louder and trench coat man flapped his arms around. That was when I recognized the short man—it was the guy who had been following me earlier; he'd just added a trench coat and a fedora. How noir!

I still couldn't hear their conversation, but I did catch a few words. Like "Not beer, you idiot!" and "Porn!"

Then the figures walked away together and disappeared out of my line of sight. I waited a while to see if they'd come back, but there was no sign of them.

This needed to stop, but I had no idea what "this" was, or how to make it end.

SIX

I stayed at the shop an extra thirty minutes past closing time. What was the rush to get home? True, I had to make sure the chickens hadn't escaped—they could've made it halfway to the Kansas border by this point in the day—but other than that, the only thing waiting for me at home was Bigfoot.

When I walked in the front door, I dumped my bag in the kitchen and made a beeline for the backyard, where I discovered all the birds were still safe and sound. When I'd fed them their dinner, I sat on the patio to assess my situation.

I couldn't help but think this was all Kelly's fault. Why had she asked me, that very day at lunch, right out of the blue, if I'd seen a Bigfoot? That had been way too weird to be a coincidence, and now she'd jinxed me. Yup, all her fault.

Even though I was mad at her for manifesting this stupid article into existence, she was also still the only person I could think of to vent to. Maybe I could have called my mom about it, but that always led to more trouble than it was worth. She'd probably ask me what I planned to wear when I interviewed Bigfoot, and make me find out if he was single. I pulled my phone out of my back pocket and dialed Kelly's number, going with the better choice.

"Darn you and your freakishly accurate clairvoyant skills!" It wasn't how I usually started a friendly conversation, but these were unusual times. The chickens stared at me nervously.

"Um, hello?" Kelly sounded confused.

"What do I do? I don't even know where to start!" I said in a half-yell after I relayed the basics of my situation to her. "What the heck!" My aggravation and solitary afternoon had left me way too much time to think about everything, and in turn that had turned me awfully cranky. It was possible I also needed a protein snack.

"Well," said Kelly in a calm voice, since she was used to my occasional anxiety-induced rants by now, "you worked in fiction for over twenty years, so this shouldn't be too much of a stretch for you, right?"

"I don't work for the *National Enquirer* for cripes' sake. I know this is a small town, but I work for a real newspaper, and last time I checked, news articles are supposed to be factual. Except if it's about politics, in which case all bets are off. But this is supposed to be serious journalism!" I slammed my fist on the patio table. Ow.

Kelly laughed.

"This is funny to you?"

"Yes," she said. "So freakin' funny."

"Not helping!"

"Okay, fine. So treat this as you would any other investigative piece. Maybe you go look up what's already been written on the topic."

"Now you're telling me how to write a newspaper article?" I asked with plenty of indignation in my voice.

"You asked."

"Oh. Right."

"Go talk to the latest round of eyewitnesses. Find a local expert or two."

"There are Bigfoot *experts*?" I asked. My insolence was about to turn into hysterical laughter.

"Oh sure," she said calmly. "Remember, Bigfoot has been an Oklahoma native for a long time. There's folks around here who know quite a bit about it all."

"Like who?" I decided then and there that I needed to meet a Bigfoot expert.

"Try Danny Cadence. He knows a lot about the local Bigfoot scene."

Danny Cadence. I made a mental note. Local Bigfoot scene. *Scene?* This time I was the one who laughed. "Any idea where can I find this Mr. Cadence? Does he live in the woods somewhere with his mother and a talking log?"

"I'm not exactly sure what he's up to these days," Kelly said with a factual air, ignoring my jab. "He lives up north of town, but Mark can track him down for you; they're friends. Oh, and you should probably talk to the sheriff. He's the one who has to field all those calls."

I laughed. "I'll bet the sheriff hangs up on the wackos who call in with a sighting."

"I doubt it," she said. "I told you, it's a thing here."

"Yes, right. A thing. A crazy thing. This is cray-*zee*!" I couldn't understand how she was staying so rational about it all.

"If you feel that way about it, why don't you write it as a fictional story? Or an exposé maybe?"

I considered her words. Choosing one of her suggestions might be my only way to get through the assignment. It might not be great journalism, but that might not matter so much—or less than I had originally hoped. "That's a possibility, I guess."

"It might not make you any friends, but at least you'd be true to your 'journalistic ethics' or whatever your problem is."

"I don't have a problem, other than I'm supposed to be

writing the truth." I frowned into the phone. "And what do you mean it won't make me any friends?"

"Like I said, people around here take Bigfoot seriously. If you make fun of them, or try to prove them wrong, you might stir up a real hornet's nest for yourself. They won't like you."

I hadn't thought of this. Mostly because I'd had no idea that slandering Bigfoot in Guthrie would be career-ending. It must have been up there on the list with OU football and fried okra. "For reals, Kelly. You're an attorney. You specialize in thoughtfully presented arguments. Tell me you don't think this is a little bit batshit crazy?"

"Not necessarily," she answered. "The world is not black and white."

"Spoken like a true lawyer," I muttered. "Okay. I appreciate your thoughts, anyway. I guess. I will take them under advisement."

"Also spoken like a true lawyer," she said, then laughed. "If the newspaper fires you for dissing Sasquatch, you could always try to pass the bar."

"Yeah, sure. Sasquatch can be my first client." I thanked Kelly and ended the call, making a mental note to contact the sheriff and to text Mark and ask him where I could find one Danny Cadence. I'd do all that later. Maybe if I waited a little longer to get started, it would all magically disappear.

All this mental anguish was making me hungry. I went into the kitchen to rustle up some food, but I ended up wandering around aimlessly because I kept forgetting why I was in there. I had moved to Oklahoma to get away from the hustle, grind, and overall freak show that was New York. I had moved here to live a simple life—to enjoy some peace and quiet, cheaper real estate, and to get some writing done without any distractions. Sasquatch was not part of my three, five, or even ten-year Life Plan.

I warmed up a bowl of my homemade potato and vegetable

soup and sat down to make some notes. The way I saw it, I had three options for approaching the story. I wrote them down so I could stare at them balefully.

- *Option 1: Write a clear, concise "news story," sticking to "the facts" from eyewitnesses and any supporting data I can find. Pros: I could keep my job and make everyone happy. Cons: I would be lying, and I'd feel like a total fraud. Because everyone knows Bigfoot isn't real.*
- *Option 2: Write an exposé proving everyone in town wrong, except for me. Pros: Personal vindication! Possible journalism award! Cons: I could disappoint the whole town, lose business at the Book Store, and probably my job at the paper.*
- *Option 3: Approach it as fiction and write a combination of options 1 and 2 in such a way that readers won't be able to tell what kind of story it is, but they'll want to keep reading it. Pros: Keep job, make people happy, be able to live with myself. Cons: I still have to write the darn thing.*

Staring at my options balefully didn't seem to help. I wanted out; it was that plain and simple. I reached for my phone and sent Mark a message under a pretext that I thought seemed plausible.

. . .

Me: *Hey have you seen my favorite pencil anywhere?*
   Mark: *no*
   Me: *Also, you were kidding about writing an article on Sasquatch, right?*
   Mark: *no*

All right, at least I tried. Unfortunately, it was now time to put together a plan for this job. But simply thinking about not being able to get out of it sent another wave of anxiety through me. At this point I contemplated breaking out an Emergency Beer from the fridge but went for the Emergency Cookies instead. It's been scientifically proven that cookies can fix darn near everything.

I would have to turn something in by Sunday night, so if I was going to do this, I needed to start interviewing and researching soon. I wondered if I was going to have to interview some of those cryptid-loving wackos. You know the ones—they believe those "home movies" of a tall guy dressed up in a furry ape suit are real, even though the quality of the film is so grainy that you couldn't tell if you were looking at a real monster or a wet mop.

My first thought was that this might be a great time to thoroughly clean my bathroom, including regrouting the tub and installing a new sink faucet. Maybe a quick search of YouTube tub-grouting videos, for inspiration. An hour later I resurfaced from the depths of the internet, undecided about bathroom projects but decidedly hungry.

While I munched on a handful of tiny cookies (because everyone knows that making them smaller means they have less calories), I had another horrible mental image of having to trim

Bigfoot's nose hairs, and that sealed the deal. I decided to go ahead and take whatever was behind Curtain Number 3. I would make my article the best darn piece of literary fiction this town had ever seen. In the immortal words of Dr. Hunter S. Thompson, *when the going gets weird, the weird turn pro.* I could do this.

I added a few more items to my to-do list and vowed to get started straight away. Tomorrow.

SEVEN

I woke up slowly on Tuesday morning, rolling over onto my side and opening my eyes to the bright early-morning sunshine. It was a glorious feeling to wake up naturally, without an alarm. I felt a few seconds of peace and satisfaction. But then, without meaning to, I thought about Bigfoot. It started with the word *Bigfoot* popping into my mind. Next I thought of all that fur. And as much I tried not to go there, I did. Now he was in bed with me. I mean, he wasn't really in bed with me (I felt around under the covers just to be sure), but he may as well have been. I could practically hear him snoring. I yawned, gave up on trying to get rid of him, and instead invited him to breakfast. We ate together in the kitchen, with very little conversation. His table manners left something to be desired.

After talking to Kelly the previous night, I had put a call in to Al Turner to set up an interview for this afternoon. We had agreed I would drive out to his place, north of town. I could do it on my lunch hour since I was the boss; I simply gave myself permission to take a longer break than usual. Julie had a full day of school, so she couldn't cover for me. It wasn't ideal to close the shop, but most of the local store owners took a little time off every once in a while, to eat or run a few errands. Even us small business moguls needed to do stuff like go to the dentist or get coffee. Or interview someone about Bigfoot. Someday, when business picked up a little more, I'd be able to afford having the shop covered the whole day long, but for now, a long lunch would do.

After a busy yet uneventful morning at the bookstore (no guys in trench coats to be seen anywhere), I packed up around noon to get going. By this time the anticipation about the interview was getting to me, so I decided I deserved a cappuccino for extra mental fortitude. I took a detour for a quick stop at Hoboken. Seth was friendly as always, not mentioning the coffee spillage incident of the day before. No sign of Mr. Cute Boots. I wasn't sure if I was disappointed or relieved.

The drive to Al Turner's place was quite pleasant, and I had been right—it was greatly enhanced by the enjoyment of a cappuccino. His property wasn't too far outside of town, but it was distant enough that the landscape changed from old buildings and small neighborhoods to rolling fields and groves of short, scrubby trees.

Every time I drove around rural Oklahoma, it surprised me how much of the horizon I could see. Especially compared to Manhattan, where the sky was only small slivers of blue, gray, or brownish-black visible between towering buildings.

But out here, the sky was big, the ground was flat, and a woman could get to feeling a little lonely. It was a good kind of lonely, though, if there was such a thing. It was the kind of lonely that made you feel disconnected from other people but very connected to the natural world around you. I sighed contentedly as I sipped my coffee. Some melancholy music would have completed the vibe, but today I opted for silence.

The rich, delicious cappuccino reminded me of what had happened at Hoboken the day before. As I watched the scenery go by, I had plenty of time to contemplate what a dork I had been. What made me turn into a tongue-tied klutz around a man? I was never like that in New York, not even in stressful business meetings and never, *ever* over a guy. I must have gotten good at keeping my defenses up—both at work and at play. It was hard to admit, but there it was. To be fair, being tough was necessary sometimes in life. But there was probably such a thing as overdoing it when it came to being defensive. It might be a good idea to remember that, now that I owned my own small business.

Yes, maybe I could soften up a bit, now that I was living out here on the prairie. I could start saying things like "Oh, bless your heart!" and make friends with my landlady. How precious! That idea lasted about five seconds. Because if softening up meant I would also act like an idiot in front of good-looking men, then I wasn't sure I wanted any part of it. *Blech!* I resolved to toughen right back up.

That Mr. Cute Boots though, what a fine piece of human engineering he was. Even if he had laughed me right out of the coffee shop. Those eyes. They could cause traffic jams—or worse. Political stalemates, union strikes, tsunamis. I wondered how many other women had spilled coffee on his boots, or had died trying. My stars, it had been a while since I'd been inspired to think these kinds of thoughts about a man. It wasn't entirely unpleasant, even if he had caused me to turn into a bona fide oaf.

Google Maps informed me that in one thousand feet I needed to turn right off the main highway and onto a smaller county street, so I slowed down to take the turn at a reasonable speed. Houses were set back from the road and situated on large pieces of land; the occasional fence delineated property lines and kept livestock from wandering. After a few more minutes, the houses became spread even farther apart.

All the deep thoughts I'd been having about making an idiot of myself in public, plus a slight caffeine buzz, had allowed me to forget I was out here to interview someone who had claimed to see a mythical beast with oversized feet. But as I pulled onto Al Turner's property, I couldn't forget any longer.

Earlier that morning, I'd tried to put together a comprehensive list of questions for my interview with Al. It hadn't taken long. What was I going to ask him besides, "Are you nuts?" I reckoned that would cover all the bases. If the interview did happen to continue a little longer, maybe I'd follow up with, "Seriously, are you nuts?" Oh heck. Forget the questions. I'd wing it.

I turned off the car and tipped the Hoboken cup to my lips one last time. Empty. Shucks. There was nothing left for me to do but face my fate.

As I walked past the gate leading to Al's backyard, I took a quick detour to check out the area behind his house. A large fenced-in chicken coop ran along one side of his yard. I heard a few soft, contented clucks and felt a little more hopeful. Chickens made everything better.

Perhaps this wouldn't be as bad as I had feared! I continued around the house toward the front door. I nearly lost my footing when a loud rustling emitted from the bushes under a large picture window.

"What the—" I yelled, trying to keep my balance. I recovered as best I could and teetered on one foot. The rustling stopped. I walked a little closer to the window, but I couldn't see anything in the dense greenery of the evergreen bushes. I stepped even closer. I looked down and saw the tip of a Velcro-closure orthopedic sandal. Attached to a man's leg clad in polyester plaid pants. They were the same ones I'd seen the day before—their green, blue, and white pattern were unforgettable. It had to be the same guy who'd been following me. Slowly, the shoe dragged along the dirt and disappeared into the bush.

"You!" I said before it occurred to me that this lurker could be dangerous. "Hey! I know you're in there so you might as well show yourself!" That was when I realized it might not have been the best move on my part to invite whoever had been following me around to join me out in the open in a stranger's yard. And the words *show yourself* might not have been the best choice, either.

It was too late now, so I hiked my bag up on my shoulder and prepared to make a run for it, just in case. "Hey!" I tried again.

Slowly the mystery person began to stand up in front of the picture window. Sure enough, it was the same guy. Black ladies' sunglasses and all.

This was so dumb. Why was I being followed by someone who clearly wasn't very good at his assignment? "What do you want?" I yelled at him.

I could tell my yelling had spooked him—a pair of bushy white eyebrows rose up above the rim of the glasses and his mouth dropped open. Before I could say anything else, he scrambled out of the bush and ran. As he tried to round the corner of the house, one of his man sandals slipped out from under him and he went skidding into the grass.

"Ooof!" he said as he landed with a thud. Clearly he wasn't much of a threat to me, so I stood where I was and watched as he made his way to all fours and very ungracefully got up to his feet again. He sped around the corner and was gone.

I wasn't sure if I was in some sort of surreal comedy sketch, or if my life had simply taken a very weird turn. I also wasn't sure if I was more mad, surprised, scared, or confused. Regardless, I was going to get some answers from Al Turner—about Bigfoot maybe, but more importantly, about whoever had been lurking in the undergrowth.

I marched toward the door when a sudden thought stopped

me in my tracks. Had that guy been Al Turner? Surely he wouldn't be lurking in his own bushes. However, this was a guy who claimed he'd seen Bigfoot, so all bets were off.

I stood still for a few seconds longer, waiting to see if anyone else popped out of the bushes, or flew off the roof maybe, but it seemed all was clear, so I made for the door. Time to get this party started.

I squared my shoulders, set my jaw, and opened the screen door. I slammed the brass door knocker against its plate and snorted as I made a mental note to use a *nice knockers* line somewhere in my book.

No one answered. I knocked again. Still nothing. I let the screen door close and was about to turn and leave when the front door creaked open. A wiry, compact septuagenarian pushed at the screen door and poked his head outside to get a better look at me. I made the assumption this was Al Turner. It was not the same white-haired man who had been in the bushes. I was relieved, but also a bit disappointed.

"There was a man in your bushes!" I blurted.

He stared at me. At least I think he was looking at me—his eyes were so squinty they were almost closed, as if this was his first exposure to sunlight in a week. His stubbled chin jutted out, and his skin was so pale I wondered if he might be a vampire. I would search online for *Guthrie vampires* in addition to *Guthrie Bigfoot* as part of the research phase for my article.

"Nuh-uh," he said, making no move to let me in.

"Yes there was! Right there!" I pointed to the picture window. He craned his neck so he could peek out farther and turn his head in the direction of the bushes.

"Nope."

I opened my mouth to say something else, but no sound came out. I had nothing.

It seemed Al was done with that particular topic, because all he did next was silently wave me in and let go of the screen door. I had to reach out quickly to catch it before it slammed in my face. Once inside, I closed the door behind me and when I turned back around, he'd already left the room and was headed down a hallway. As he walked, he held up his right hand and waved it around. I made the executive decision to interpret it as an invitation for me to follow.

"So, um, you have chickens, huh?" I asked the back of his head. Silence. I didn't let it discourage me. "I got some a couple months ago. Aren't they great?" More silence. Like those yoga people always tell you to do, I let it go, and we continued to meander down the hall in silence.

"Damn noisy things, always trying to get out," the back of Al's head finally griped as it and the rest of his body entered the kitchen. It took me a second to figure out what he was talking about, because my mind had already wandered to a new topic: sandwiches.

And here I thought all this time that everyone loved chickens! This was the second indication that something must have been wrong with him. The first was that he had claimed to see Bigfoot. Two strikes already.

He sat down at a small table in the corner of his kitchen. He looked like he might fall asleep sitting up; his eyes were still squinty, and he let out a big yawn which he didn't bother covering up. He groped for a nearby mug and started taking big gulps of whatever was in it. What could it have been? Coffee? Rocket fuel? Pepto?

He motioned for me to sit and began to smooth out the wrinkles in the blue-and-white check tablecloth. It had a stain on it which I hoped was spaghetti sauce. A pile of bills lay in the center of the table, and a few opened beer cans sat next to the pile. You could tell a lot about a man by what was on his kitchen table—and embedded in the tablecloth.

I sat down in the only other chair and it creaked as I settled myself. I made a mental note to perhaps go on a diet. I then pretended to rummage through my bag looking for my notebook and pencil. I knew I was stalling, but I hadn't come up with any other questions other than the two I'd thought of that morning.

I pulled out my writing gear and my phone and turned on its recording app.

"You're not going to tell me about the guy in the bushes?" I asked.

"What guy?" asked Al.

"The guy who, who..." I made a half-hearted effort to point down the hall. "The guy?"

Al stared at me again, one hand holding the mug, the other resting on his knee. "So you're new to the paper, are ya?" he asked, cocking his head to one side to get a better look at me through what must have been his good eye.

"Yes, that's right. I've been at the *Ledger* about three months now," I answered politely.

"I used to work there. Did your hotshot fancypants editor ever tell you that?"

"No, he didn't," I said, pretending to write something down. I could feel a doodle coming on. A good one.

"Yup. I used to work up on the second floor, as a layout editor." He took a few more gulps from his mug, a slight flush now entering his cheeks. I wondered again what was in the mug and if I could have some too. It might make this train wreck go faster. Or at least take away some of the pain.

"Oh really," I said. The tone of his voice made me think there was a bona fide story behind his statement. I also had a feeling that the story didn't have a happy ending, hence the term *hotshot fancypants editor*. Ordinarily I'd love a distraction like this, but today I wanted out and my intuition told me Al was about to launch into a major opus about his time at the paper. I was going to have to think fast before this small topic detour became a major rerouting. Maybe I would ask Mark about it later when I got back. Maybe.

"Oh yes, right," I recalled quickly. "I think I remember hearing about that now. Mark asked me not to talk about it, though. It's all confidential. Legal considerations and whatnot." I tapped the side of my nose with my index finger and then wondered what in the world had made me do it.

Al didn't say anything, but he had a confused look on his face which I suspected wasn't going anywhere anytime soon unless I tried for another subject change.

"So. About your alleged Bigfoot sighting on Sunday," I said. "Where were you when you supposedly saw the fictional creature?"

"Oh, for cryin' out loud!" said Al as he leaned back and crossed his legs at the knee, mug still in hand. He must have finally woken up. "You know as well as I do that Bigfoot isn't fictional—he's real!" He lowered his head to look at me as if he were trying to peer over a pair of reading glasses. However, there were no glasses anywhere on his head.

I pretended not to hear this last remark. "So this allegedly happened sometime on Saturday? Or was it Sunday?" My pen was poised over my notebook, ready to write down the next words out of his mouth, which I was sure would be fascinating.

"It was Saturday night. Or maybe technically Sunday morning." He scratched his temple. "Or was it Friday? No, pretty sure it was Saturday. I mean Sunday."

I wrote a big question mark in my notebook. It was definitely time to start doodling.

"Me and Bill—that's Bill Turner, my cousin Bill—we'd gone over to Cedar Valley to visit our other cousin Frank. Frank Turner." He tried to take a look at my notebook, as if wanting to make sure I knew how to spell TURNER.

So far, I was managing to keep up. *Al. Bill. Frank. Turner.*

"You saw this thing over in Cedar Valley?" I asked. I continued writing. *Cedar Valley.*

"Nope." He got up from the table and poured himself a

glass of water from a pitcher by the sink. He set the glass back down on the table next to his mug, and I suddenly realized I was incredibly thirsty. Sadly, he went on without offering me a glass. "After me and Bill left Frank's place, I took Bill back to his house. In my truck. That one out there." He nodded his head toward the kitchen window, and I could see an old Ford Ranger truck parked alongside the house. I didn't give a flying flip about the truck but finally decided to write *drove in truck—Ford Ranger* in my notebook so I would look busy.

"As I was driving to Bill's, that's when we saw him."

"Bill saw it, too?"

"Oh yeah, for sure he did. In fact, Bill saw him first. It was him what yelled out, 'Hey look, there's Bigfoot!'"

"How do you know it was a male?" I regretted asking it as soon as the words left my mouth.

"Well now." Al's face brightened considerably, and he leaned in toward me. Oh no. This was not a good sign. I leaned back, trying to keep distance between us.

"That's a very good question!" he continued. "I read the other day about the physical differences between male and female Sasquatches, based on some charts from the most recent data—"

"So you saw this thing, in the middle of the night, clearly enough to determine that its physical attributes fell into an acceptable range of your questionable data that led you to determine it was a male specimen?"

"Huh?" Al's jaw dropped open slightly, and he narrowed his eyes.

"How exactly could you tell it was male?" I tried again.

"Oh, that's easy. The lady Bigfoots always stay hidden. They're shy, you know." Al leaned back in his chair again with an air of professorial knowledge regarding the gender characteristics of Sasquatches.

"All right, sure. So anyway..." I may have come across as a

little too snarky, but goshdarnit, this was getting to be too much. I had to do something right quick, before he started showing me Bigfoot charts. But I was too late.

Al had turned around in his seat and pulled a stack of papers off the counter behind him, which he now held in his two unsteady hands. "In fact," he said, "if we review the most recent statistics, I'd say that based on the height of the subject and the width of the shoulders, we was definitely looking at a male specimen." He set the papers on the table, licked the tip of his bony index finger, and peeled off the top three pages of the messy stack. Then he thought better of it and shoved the entire pile at me. He pointed at a graph on the top page, trying to read it upside down.

It didn't appear that he was going to continue talking to me unless I inspected his "research," so I reached for my phone and snapped a photo of the entire piece of paper and shuffled through the rest of the stack, pretending to be interested.

"Oh, hmm, I see, yes," I said as I looked at a few more sheets. He seemed pleased with this. I set the papers down on the table and assumed we were clear to move on. "Okay, so anyway, you allegedly saw the thing at your cousin Bill's place?"

Al scratched the side of his head, making the snow-white, wiry hair stand straight out. It made him look even more off balance than I knew he already was.

"Huh." He looked off in the distance, toward the refrigerator, which, right on cue, began to make a truly horrible noise. It sounded like he had a Bigfoot in there. He still hadn't continued talking. Yup, it definitely sounded like there was a Bigfoot in the fridge and I was afraid it was going to start shimmying across the kitchen floor any second. I took a deep breath and started to count backward from a thousand.

Finally Al went on. "Like I said, it was Bill what saw Bigfoot first. We came to a sharp turn in the road, about a quarter mile before you get to the house." He made a curvy wave through the air with his left hand. "There's a big tree there, I think it's oak. Wait a sec, let me check." He turned around again and reached for a *Trees of North America* guidebook. Oh snap. Next he was going to tell me what the temperature and humidity level had been.

"But it's an area you're familiar with?" I was desperate to get back on track now.

"Oh yeah! Like the back of my hand, dontcha know." He looked down at the palm of his right hand before slowly turning it over to inspect the back of it too.

"And?" I tried to look riveted by the story and I poised my pencil over my notebook again.

"And we was driving pretty fast—I like to drive fast." He flashed me a huge grin. "Anyway, the headlights caught a big brown blob over in the tree line. Bill says, 'There's Bigfoot!' and sure as god's got sandals, there he was!"

I drew an X across the entire page of my notebook and put my pen down gingerly on the table before I got tempted to stab Al in the eye with it. I figured I'd go ahead and ask a few more questions, though, to fill in my fictional account for the paper.

"So he was brown? How long was his hair?" I asked.

"Yup, this one was a rich chocolatey brown. They can range from brown to gray, depending on the season," he said, once again giving the appearance of someone who was very confident about their Bigfoot facts. "Same with length of hair. It gets longer in the winter 'cause they get cold. Then they molt in the spring."

Oh, this was too much fun. I was getting such good stuff for my novel—I mean newspaper article. "Al," I said politely, smiling my best friendly Oklahoma smile at him, "you weren't by any chance drinking that night, were you?"

"Ah, well, there *may* have been a few beers involved. Yeah, I guess I'd had a couple, I suppose. I didn't have my glasses on either. But none of that don't make no difference—I saw him!"

He squirmed in his chair and for a second his expression turned sad. "When I drove back to Bill's later Sunday morning, I looked and looked and couldn't find any trace of him. But I tell you what, we saw that big hairy beast Saturday night, all right!" He suddenly waved his hands in the air, becoming more animated.

"Okay," I said, trying to placate him. "Sure, sure. And you didn't have your glasses with you, while you were driving home in the dark after having a few beers?"

"Right. I forgot my glasses at Bill's place when I picked him up earlier that night. Happens more than I'd care to admit, but don't worry. I drive without those dang things all the time."

"Uh-huh. I'm relieved to hear it," I said under my breath. "And why did you drive back to Bill's the next morning?"

"To get my glasses, of course! I can't see for crap without these things." Al started to push his imaginary specs farther up his nose before he realized they weren't there. He felt the top of his head, then looked around the kitchen helplessly. I knew I should help Al look for them, but I wanted to make it home before the weekend, so I chose not to notice. I did have an epiphany though—if I ever saw Al Turner's truck out on the road, I would call the sheriff's department immediately and take cover in the nearest ditch.

"That's just super, Al. Thanks so much for your time." I closed my notebook and got up from the table. "I think I have everything I need here."

"D'you want to take my picture or anything? For the paper?" He got up too, and ran a hand through his hair, making it stand on end even more.

"I'll let you know. If we need a photo, we'll send someone out from the paper. A photographer."

"Sure thing, missy," said Al, who tried to straighten his wrinkled pearl snap shirt.

"And you don't want to tell me anything about the guy in your bushes?" I wanted to give him one last chance.

"Nope," he said.

"Okay then, I guess I'll call the Sheriff's Department and report a suspicious person hanging around your house. I wouldn't want anything to happen to you, after all." I waited to see what he would say to that.

Nothing, apparently.

It became obvious he wasn't going to show me out, so I walked down the hall toward the front door on my own. "Thanks again," I called out. No response.

When I passed through the living room, I happened to spy Al's glasses on the floor. I picked them up and placed them on the small console table by the front door and let myself out. I walked outside into the fresh afternoon air. I peered at the bushes as I walked back to my car, but there was no sign of anyone.

EIGHT

I made it back to the bookstore and reopened just in time for a massive crowd of one mom and three kids to come in. I loved kids—as long as they were someone else's. There was probably a very good reason that universal forces had skipped over me when it came to maternal instincts, thereby keeping me out of the gene pool. I never questioned the fact that it hadn't been in the cards for me. Who was I to question universal forces?

There were exceptions to almost every rule, but for the most part, kids were adorable. As far as children in my bookstore went, it was hit or miss. It would always go one of two ways: either the kids would tear up the store and no one would buy anything, or alternatively, they would tear up the store and the parents would buy something so at least I'd get compensated for having to spend an hour putting the picture books section back together.

Today I was lucky enough to experience the latter scenario. Theresa Highsmith brought in her two daughters and one of their friends to pick out a few chapter books. I had met Theresa the month before, when she brought Bree and Becca in for Saturday Storytime, and we got to talking about romance novels.

Books always brought people together! Sometimes I wished we could start a big ol' Book Club of the World and throw politics out the window, instead choosing to bond over shared stories. Maybe someday. I was hopeful.

Having three energetic youngsters running around the store was a great distraction from thinking about my impending article assignment. I considered inviting them to stay longer and maybe ordering a pizza to be delivered so that I could procrastinate even more. But alas, I knew that would be pushing it. And it would also be kind of weird. So when my customers were ready to leave, I begrudgingly let them.

I sat down behind the counter and took out my reporter's notebook. I was shocked—*shocked!*—to discover that there still wasn't much in there that I could use. I listened to the recording I made of my interview with Al. Nothing there, either. Geez, this was going to be tricky. Even though I'd already decided to approach the whole thing as fiction, it was still going to take a few artistic liberties to make this work. Normally I wouldn't take any such freedoms with a journalism piece, but desperate times called for desperate measures.

Before I could think of anything brilliant, however, I was going to need nourishment. I was starving. My mind wandered to sandwiches again, and from there it was a short memory jog back to that great deli on Fifth Avenue in Manhattan and their specialty sandwich minus the onions. I wondered if they were still open. Maybe I should google it. Did Mr. Cute Boots like sandwiches? If he was against mayo, our love affair would never work. Ugh, work.

I couldn't find my way out of my thoughts. Like the cartoon rabbit of way back when, I had missed that left turn at Albuquerque, and I couldn't navigate my way back onto the freeway of normal thought. I was starting to think I might become lost forever, when the door to my shop opened and my dad walked in.

"Hi hi, sweetie pie!" he said brightly. It was how he'd greeted me for as long as I could remember. The sight of him in my store and the childhood phrase acted like a switch, turning on the driver-assist software of my consciousness. I was instantly jerked back into my lane. It gave me whiplash, but I was no longer out of control and careening down the Great Rumble Strip of Life.

"Hi, Popster!" I said. He hated it when I called him Popster. But I couldn't resist. "Where's the Monster?" Oops! It wasn't the first time I'd made that Freudian slip and probably wouldn't be the last.

"She's parking the car," he said, seeming not to have noticed my error. Or if he had, he was okay with it. Hard to say.

He walked over to one of the front display tables and looked over the titles. Or at least I think that's what he was doing. He squinted his eyes and leaned in so close to the new Michael Connelly novel that I thought he might try to lick it.

"Please don't eat that," I said to him.

He looked up at me, but before he could say anything, the door opened again and in came my mom.

"Beverley, you need to clean those front windows. They're filthy!"

"Hi to you, too, Mom," I responded, trying to sound cheery. I had no idea what they were doing here. Usually their visits coincided with some natural disaster or bad news or at the very least a volley of criticisms tossed my way, so I was wary.

"We were driving through on our way home from Okarche," she said, using her scary mom skills to read my mind. She absently ran her hand along the counter and looked at the tips of her fingers to check for dust. We all knew that Guthrie wasn't anywhere on the route from Okarche back to OKC, but we all chose to ignore this fact. "You know how your father is about that diner with the fried chicken," she added in a disapproving tone.

"Still the best, Dad?" I asked.

"Still the best," he answered, patting his belly. A quiet burp emerged from his mouth, and he smiled. My mom smacked him on the arm as she walked by, and I tried not to laugh.

"Too bad you've eaten, or I'd invite you over to Stacy's Place for a sandwich," I said, frowning a little but just for show. On the inside I was secretly relieved they weren't hungry. I wasn't in the mood to entertain them through a whole meal, what with Bigfoot and all.

"That's okay, dear. We're positively *stuffed*," my mom said. "But we'd love to see how you've come along with your house. Isn't it time for you to close up?" She looked around for the nonexistent clock.

They had sprung a home visit on me only a few weeks earlier, interrupting a major bookshelf reorganization. I didn't know if she was expecting me to have completely remodeled since then, or maybe added an extra wing to my rental house, but clearly she thought it still needed improvement.

"I'd love to visit with you guys, but I have a really big story I'm working on for the paper right now. I'm afraid it's going to eat up all my spare time for the next few weeks," I said.

When I'd first landed back in Oklahoma, I had moved in with my parents in Oklahoma City. I stayed with them as their house guest, sleeping in my old room. It was like being in high school again, and I almost had to sneak out the window a few times, like the good old days. In a short time, I was once again trained in the art of trying to avoid a million questions about where I was going and who I was seeing, and ignoring instructions to take my can of mace wherever I went. I couldn't tell you how many times I heard the phrase, *Be careful out there because you never know*—both when I was young, and earlier this year.

I had been considering staying in Oklahoma City, in case my mom and dad needed me as they got older. But within ten minutes of unpacking my bags, I decided it would be a very bad idea to live too close. Maybe even the same city would be inadvisable. Or possibly even anywhere within a three-state radius. They meant well, but you'd be hard-pressed to find two people more disappointed in my love life than they were. Subtlety wasn't their strong suit.

They'd wanted to see me married, with kids and a nice husband and a dog and a lifestyle blog. They rarely missed an opportunity to let me know I was letting them down. My younger sister Emily had all of those things, and my parents were happy about it, but they wanted me to be the same as her. But the older I got, the more I didn't want to fit into that mold, or any mold for that matter. God love them, but they didn't get it.

When I gave up my publishing job in New York, they thought I had completely lost my mind, and before I'd packed my first moving box, they'd already offered to pay for counseling. I was tempted to take the money and spend it on booze, but I thought that might prove them right.

If I'd stayed with them much longer in their house, I definitely would have been driven to drink. I politely declined their offer for therapy and blind-date setups and immediately began looking for someplace farther away to live. After a few visits to Guthrie, I had fallen in love. Now here I was, a bookstore owner and reporter, and still wary every time my parents came to visit.

My mom stopped milling around the front of the store and came to stand in front of me, one hand on her hip, the other crossed in front of her waist.

"Honestly, Beverley," she scolded. "I don't know why you keep yourself so busy. How do you find time to get anything done at home? How will you ever find time to *date?*"

There it was. It had taken her approximately three minutes

to press one of my buttons. I took a deep breath and tried to count to five. I made it to two.

"Look, Mom, I appreciate your concern. But I'm fine. I have plenty of free time, and I love both of my jobs and everything else just the way it is. I don't want to date anyone right now. I am perfectly capable of being by myself." I could feel my temples starting to throb.

She shook her head and made those *tsk* sounds we all loathe to hear, especially when they're directed at us. "You're not getting any younger," she pointed out. "You should think this through, you know? You're running out of *time*, Beverley."

When I was little, my mom would tell me that I acted before "thoroughly thinking things through." She told me this on a regular basis. Like, a million times a day. She had probably been telling me this since the day I was born, which was three weeks earlier than everyone had been planning for. I'm sure she held me responsible for that too.

This particular admonition started bothering me when I hit those wonderful teenage years. Because when you're sixteen, you know everything, your parents are idiots, and everything they say is *wrong*, and who are they to tell you anything about yourself, anyway, what do they know?

And the last thing your teenage self wants is for a kernel of truth to come out of the mouth of your mother. It was then that I started doing things without thinking them through on purpose. Nothing major, like I didn't burn down a grocery store or join the Young Republicans or anything like that. But if it was harmless and I knew it would bug my mom, I would do it.

My rebellious streak continued past my teenage years, as did my propensity to act quickly. When I was about thirty, I was finally willing to acknowledge that maybe my mom could be kind of right. A little bit. Sometimes. Possibly. It occurred to me around that age that this behavior—acting without thinking things through—could explain a lot about where I was in my life and what was happening in it. Or what wasn't happening.

Making quick, intuitive decisions had come in handy in the publishing industry. I'd found a lot of great authors, and made a lot of money, by using this approach. But it also explained why I had a lot of never-worn clothes in my closet, a few (very large) regrets in the romance department, and a tenuous relationship with my mother.

Now in my forties, I was starting to learn. I'm not saying I didn't make quick decisions anymore, but I was able to think things through faster, and I definitely knew what I wanted in life more now than when I was younger. I could trust my intuition more, too. I was the quintessential late bloomer, but at least I was blooming. And I wished my mom would give me a freaking break already. Sometimes she made me so mad I wanted to stab the back of my hand with a ... a ... a stabby thingy. But no. Because with my newfound wisdom, I was smart enough to know the right thing to do in a situation such as this.

I sighed and walked over to stand next to my mother, putting my arm around her shoulder. "Mom," I said softly. "I'm okay. Everything is fine, and everything is the way I want it to be. Now, would you guys like to join me for tea at the coffeehouse before you head home?"

She frowned at me, but it only lasted a few seconds. Her gaze softened, and she spoke quietly like I had. "No thanks, dear, we're fine. I should probably get your father home. He forgot his glasses and has been running into things all afternoon."

And right on cue, we heard a loud crash from the back of the store that sounded a lot like a ton of books hitting the floor.

"Sorry!" My dad's voice trailed up to where we were standing.

"It's okay, Dad," I called back.

"Dear, it's time for us to leave. Beverley has lots of work to do," my mom yelled. She gave me one last worried look, and I shot one back that said *Really, I'm fine. Trust me.* We both smiled.

My dad wandered back up to the front of the store, and we were standing by the door when we heard another giant crash. This one came from the roof.

"It wasn't me!" my dad said as he threw up his hands in innocence.

Mom smacked his arm again. "Oh, don't be silly, Steve. We know it wasn't you." She turned to face me. "Beverley, you should complain about the noise to your landlord. How can you have a nice quiet place for people to read with all that banging around up there?"

"Don't worry, Mom. That's just some guys fixing the roof. They'll be done soon."

"Your roof needs fixing? What kind of dump is this? I hope you've asked for a reduction on your rent."

"I've got it covered, Mom."

"Okay, but honestly, Bev, you shouldn't take any shit from anyone, ever." She pointed her finger at me.

My eyebrows shot up in surprise. I couldn't think of what to say to that, so I stayed silent and shrugged. Suddenly I pictured my mom and Leona going at it over rent reduction and repair negotiations. I made a mental note to ask my mom to be my representative the next time I needed something from my landlady.

We said our goodbyes and they left. Upon reflection, it had gone reasonably well. Maybe there was hope.

A few minutes later, the roof guys came in and assured me all was superduper up top, and I thanked them and reminded them to send the bill to Leona. I felt totally in control of everything. But it didn't last long. Back to the Sasquatch Problem.

I considered up and quitting the paper. A great short-term

plan, but a crappy long-term one. If the topic of Bigfoot was that important to this town, I'd definitely be doing myself a disservice by refusing to take it on and leaving. Nope, I was stuck with it. I intended to spend the rest of the afternoon starting the article, but instead I drew a whole lot of little blob shapes on three pages of my reporter's notebook before finally calling it quits and heading home.

NINE

That night I tried the writing thing again. I sat down in front of my computer with my notebook, but the "BIGFOOT.DOCX" file remained blank except for my name and today's date.

Because I am a master procrastinator, I managed to fill a fair amount of time by looking online for what I would call "supporting facts," but in reality they were nothing more than cheesy websites made by Sasquatch crackpots. I did discover a few interesting—or maybe entertaining—things, however.

For example, it turned out that legends of a "large, simian-like creature" were prevalent throughout American folklore. Most alleged sightings had been in the Pacific Northwest, and the word *Sasquatch* was a derivative of the word *Sásq'ets*, from the Halkomelem language of British Columbia. I wanted to know what the heck Halkomelem was, but that would have to wait for another day. My procrastination did have (a few) limits.

Another useful tidbit worth noting: while most Bigfoot sightings were in the PNW, there had in fact been multiple sightings reported in Oklahoma. Which at least backed up the fantastical stories of a few loopy Guthrie residents. I also discovered the "Honobia Bigfoot Festival and Conference," held each fall in Honobia, Oklahoma. It was way down in the southeastern part of the state. I took solace in the fact that Mark hadn't sent me down there to cover that hayride. Yet, at least. Or maybe that was *yeti*?

I poked around the Honobia Bigfoot Organization's website, checking out this year's guest speakers which included two "doctors," a film footage expert, and someone who became obsessed after experiencing his own Bigfoot encounter. I was intrigued by the opportunity for *campling* at the festival site, thinking this might be some sort of glamorous Bigfoot yurt-type experience. Like they would prepare roasted squirrel for me, but it would be served in a Le Creuset Dutch oven. I was beyond disappointed when I learned that the mysterious *campling* offer was simply a typo and I was only welcome to plain old camping. Roasted squirrel on a stick. Meh.

The festival organizers had created a scholarship program, raising money for local high school students to attend college. I could see it clearly—the *summa cum laude* of Oklahoma State University thanking Bigfoot during her valedictorian speech.

I wondered what the people who attended the Honobia Bigfoot Festival and Conference might look like. In my mind's eye, I saw lots of flannel. And beer bellies. And beer. Plenty of roasted squirrel.

Us normal people knew it was all a hoax, but there seemed to be quite a large number of wackos—I mean, fine upstanding citizens—out there who took this stuff this very, very seriously. One could even argue, *too* seriously. Perhaps they were all as drunk and nearsighted as Al Turner, or maybe they had some sort of mental deficiency that left them devoid of all reason and logic. And weren't they afraid of this monstery beast? I couldn't be the only one!

But after spending an hour online, I came to the conclusion that everyone else in the world was honoring Bigfoot, or looking for one, or writing erotica about one. It seemed I was in the minority, not only in Guthrie, but globally. If everyone found out I was afraid of them, that might be one more way I'd be stuck in outsider limbo with no way out.

I thought again about Al and the stack of papers that was his "supporting evidence." I was in a real bind. My star Sasquatch witness had been driving drunk without his glasses, and had seen a big brown blob at a turn in the road. Let's face it—that big brown blob could have been anything. It could have been a deer. Or a big piece of meatloaf. Or maybe Al's retina detached while he was driving. More than likely, it had simply been a shadow. Or a big fat nothing at all.

It was getting late now, and I still hadn't gotten anything written, but in an attempt to further the project I told myself I'd make one phone call. But to whom? Leona Tisdale? Bill Turner? The sheriff? I finally decided on Mark. I wasn't looking forward to it, but I dreaded calling him less than anyone else on my list.

Yes, perhaps I should relay my new findings to Mark, in hopes he would tell me that on second thought, I should skip the whole stupid thing. The reality of the situation led me to believe he wasn't going to give a rat's patootie about the sobriety of my main source, and would tell me to write it anyway. Nonetheless, I felt compelled to try.

I walked around the living room a few times, trying to come up with something to say besides "Please don't make me!"

That dumb saying about eating a frog popped into my head. You know, the one that implies you should be all proactive and productive and smart and everything. Do that one thing that needs to be done. I laughed at myself for simply managing to *think* of something so practical. It must have been left over from those days when I was into my (short-lived) phase of productivity and creating good habits and setting goals and junk like that. If I were truly eating the frog, I'd sit down and start writing the confounded article already. Maybe tonight I was only eating the frog legs. Which reminded me, I still hadn't done anything about making dinner yet.

If there was any occasion that warranted an Emergency Beer, it was this one. I pulled a bottle out of the fridge and dialed Mark's number before I could talk myself out of it.

"Ellison."

I was pretty sure his cell phone had shown him who was calling and he knew it was me. But I bet that was how he answered every single time, to save a few seconds and avoid emotion and any extraneous verbal pleasantries. I pictured him answering this way when his grandma would call, or his proctologist.

"Hi, Mark. It's Beverley," I said brightly.

Nothing but silence on the other end.

"Beverley Green," I added.

"Uh-huh."

I was reminded again of how much he had changed since we were in eighth grade. Oh, how jaded some of us get. "Yeah, so, hi. Um, how are you?"

"Busy."

"Okay, sorry to disturb you. So yeah, um, I think we need to trash the Bigfoot idea. See, here's the thing—"

"No."

"Yeah, but our main witness—"

"Not trashing it."

"Well then, I'm going to need some more time to get it—"

"Nope. Sunday night."

His voice was smooth and sultry, a bit rough, and a little smoky. I wondered what I could have interrupted that made him sound so likeable. But sadly, that sexy voice wasn't saying any words I was wanting to hear. I tried one more time.

"Okay, but Al Turner was—"

"Sunday."

It looked like he wasn't going to give me a chance to tell him that Al had seen a giant piece of meatloaf the other night. There was no effing chance I could get a reprieve at this point, let alone an extension. It also looked like I wasn't even going to get to try my last-ditch effort of giving him a fake excuse. Which was just fine, since I hadn't come up with one yet.

It had been worth a try. On to the next item of business. I was going to have to break down and try for another favor.

"Okay, so in that case, like, where can I find a guy named Danny Cadence? Someone said you were friends with him."

"Danny? Why do you want to talk to Danny?" Mark sounded genuinely curious now, and I was thankful he'd finally used a sentence that had more than three words in it.

"I heard he knows a lot about Bigfoot," I said. I could hear Mark trying to cover the phone before he started laughing. He didn't quite make it. At least he was lightening up a bit, even if it was at my expense. "Look," I admitted. "I'm getting desperate here."

"Okay, okay," said Mark, his tone slightly softer. "I'll tell him you're looking for him, and I'll get back to you." He hung up without another word.

"'Kay, thanks, bye!" I yelled at the darkened screen of my phone. That big jerk! I muttered some choice curse words under my breath and took a big giant swig of my Emergency Beer. This article better earn me some points in this town or I was going to be hopping mad.

TEN

Things hadn't been going so great this week, and that was an understatement. I woke up before the proverbial buttcrack of dawn on Wednesday, right after having another nightmare about Bigfoot making me clip his toenails. There was no way I could go back to sleep after such a restless night so I went with it and found myself fed, coffeed, and at the shop by eight.

I was surprisingly productive in those two hours before the store opened. I didn't get any writing done—novel or article— but I got a lot of dusting and realphabetizing accomplished. Not very exciting, I know. But such was the glamorous life of a bookstore owner. Realphabetizing was a Zen task; I could let my mind wander, but not too far.

Today I hoped to catch a glimpse of the UPS guy as a sort of conciliatory prize. Granted, he wasn't half as intriguing or sparkly as the mystery man from Hoboken, but I was in the kind of mood where I would take what I could get.

Mike the UPS guy and I had a good relationship, even though he left boxes outside my front door when I wasn't there. But he was a very nice person, and I was somewhat forgiving, so we made it work. I looked forward to the days he delivered the goods, so to speak.

He was ruggedly good-looking in a muscled, box-lifting kind of way, and I could picture him on the cover of a romance novel, his brown shirt unbuttoned to his hairless navel, one arm resting on a hand truck stacked with boxes, the other wrapped around the waist of a windswept, bodice-ripped, hot brunette who was obviously a sexy bookstore owner.

I once had the idea to use my frustration at his propensity to abandon boxes on my doorstep as a plot for a romance novel. I wanted to call it *Spanking the UPS Man*, and the log line would be something like, *He kept putting his package in all the wrong places, and she wanted to punish him for it.* I had written it down on my notepad but never got back to it.

At ten o'clock sharp, I opened my doors to let in all my adoring fans. Which this morning consisted of the mail carrier bringing bills, and a very nice gentleman who was looking for a copy of "Roger's Thesis." I kept asking him to repeat the title, and he kept insisting it was "Roger's Thesis." At one point we ended up in a staring contest across the counter until I realized this wasn't going to get me a sale. So after a few more rounds of verbal wrangling and some vague hand gesturing, I handed him a copy of *Roget's Thesaurus* and he handed me his credit card, and we both declared victory.

I was still waiting to hear back from Mark with information about his Bigfoot expert friend, so I worked on my marketing plan for the Book Store. I wasn't fond of spending much time online, unlike those Infernal Young People who went everywhere with their eyes glued to their phones. But I wasn't a total technophobe, either, like those Infernal Old People who threw their hands up in the air, exclaimed "I can't keep up with all this shit!" and contracted a bad case of technological amnesia, suddenly forgetting how to use the TV remote.

I prided myself as being quintessentially GenX—one foot in

the digital world and one in the analog world. We were caught between the Baby Boomers and the Millennials and ignored by marketers. We flew under the radar most of the time and truth be told, I was happy to fly under the radar. My biggest beef with being a woman of "a particular age" was that no one made a decent pair of reasonably priced pants for fortysomething women. But the positive aspects of being ignored by politicians, pharmaceutical companies, and phone service providers were infinite.

We Xers also had the unique ability to bridge the gap between traditional media and newer forms of marketing and promotion. So when I sat down to brainstorm ways to increase business at my bookstore, I had a lot of tools at my disposal. I just had to figure out which ones would work best in Guthrie. This town was an unusual mix of old and new, so my planning had to be mixed, too.

I took out yet another notebook and started writing down ideas. Print ads in the *Ledger*. An Instagram account. A website geared to tourists and also locals. I was on a roll. And when I realized I was on a roll, that made me hungry and I decided I needed a roll. I deserved a hearty "I am the boss" lunch at Stacy's Place. When Julie came in for her shift, I lit out for the restaurant.

I didn't snag my regular Monday booth, but I did get one in the back, where it was quiet and I could read while I enjoyed my boss babe lunch. I made myself comfortable and pulled out my e-reader. I was in the middle of a novel that was surprisingly not a romance, or even chick lit. It was crime fiction—*Faceless Killers* by Henning Mankell. A little Nordic noir was a great counterpoint to romance novels, and it was always fun to read books that took place in foreign landscapes. There was nothing like icy weather, a meager four hours of daylight, and a bunch of dead bodies to make you appreciate the flowery happy ending of the typical romance novel.

Plus, I kind of had a thing for those noir heroes. You know—the strong, silent type with the hard exterior shell and soft, vulnerable underbelly who solved mysteries in their intense, quiet way. Noir heroes worked hard and loved hard, and there was something about them that made me swoon a little. They had flaws, sometimes big ones. But who didn't? Those flaws cost them dearly on occasion, but the noir hero always managed to do the right thing in the end. Because they had integrity and a strong, manly jawline.

I changed up my usual lunch order, and instead of getting my beloved chicken salad sandwich, I went with a salad and a BALT minus the B. I wasn't vegetarian (obviously), but sometimes I liked to feel cool and progressive and extra healthy, so on occasion I would go meat-free. *Vegetarian* was probably not a word used often in a restaurant like Stacy's, so when I wanted a healthier alternative, I had to find workarounds that people could understand, hence the subtraction of the B from my BALT. Had I ordered a "veggie sandwich" I might have gotten blank stares.

After I ordered, and drank some iced tea, I settled in and continued to read my book, stopping only long enough to thank Bonnie when she brought my food, and to take a giant bite of my sandwich.

I was so engrossed in my Nordic noir that I didn't pay enough attention to my sandwich-eating strategy, and the next time I bit into it a big glob of avocado smooshed out from between the slices of bread, made a brief stop on my lower lip, and landed squarely on the screen of my e-reader with a moist *smack*. It was a major eating fail, and an absolutely gigantic eating-in-public fail. When I looked around to see if anyone had witnessed my faux pas, I noticed Mr. Cute Boots at the door of the restaurant.

I quickly tried to duck my head, hoping he wouldn't see me, but alas, it was too late. Our eyes met across the room, which would have been romantic if I hadn't just experienced a sandwich catastrophe. His gaze held a slight hint of mischief, while I suspected my expression had more of a deer-in-headlights quality. And I probably still had a blob of avocado somewhere on my face. He also might have smiled at me, but I couldn't be sure and I didn't feel like checking at this point. I searched for my napkin, which had disappeared into thin air.

I maintained a faint glimmer of hope that he hadn't recognized me and that I would find my napkin and be able to eat the rest of my lunch in peace. I used my finger to try to wipe the food off my lip, and as I raised my head, I came face-to-waist with Mr. Cute Boots' shiny silver belt buckle. He had snuck up on me and was standing right beside my table. It was a nice belt buckle, and I felt a little better knowing he believed so strongly in secure pants. I looked up, hoping against all odds that there was no more avocado on my visage.

His hair still looked windblown, like before. He must have read my thoughts, because he reached up and ran a hand through his messy, curly hair. My insides felt wobbly. It could have been from lack of protein, but I doubted it. That bastard. He was working it. I knew it, and he knew that I knew it, and he was obviously okay with it. He gave his head a quick toss, his curls bouncing back to their usual messiness. It was his trademark move, I reckoned, and he already knew it was my weakness. And he knew it had worked. That *bastard*.

As if all that wasn't bad enough, his blue eyes were sparkling at me. For crying out loud, whose eyes actually sparkled in real life? I'd been reading schlocky lines like that in books for years, but before I'd met him, I hadn't realized it was an actual thing. And that it would make me wobbly. I could feel myself blushing again. What was next? Were my nether-regions going to start tingling? Great googlymoogly. If that was going to happen, they could at least have the decency to wait until I got home. I pleaded to all the angels that I didn't still have lunch on my face. I wished he would leave before the tingling set in.

Then I recalled our meeting the day before, in Hoboken. He had laughed at me! I didn't know for sure he had been laughing at me, but it sure seemed like he was. That big jerk! And now he was here getting a close-up view of my avocado incident. Not cool, Mr. Cute Boots, not cool.

Neither of us said anything for what seemed like forever, until I figured I might as well get it over with.

"Can I help you?" I asked in an annoyed tone. I kept looking around for a napkin and coming up empty-handed. The whole state of Oklahoma seemed to be out of them.

"No," he answered. He held out a napkin to me, having conjured one up out of the ether. I looked up at him again, and the sparkle in his eyes spread to include an equally sparkly smile. He was the napkin whisperer; it was the only explanation.

I grabbed the tissue and tried to wipe my mouth as casually as possible. "Do you mind?" I tried to look around his wonderfully proportioned body toward the door. "You're blocking my light." I smiled at him like I had a stomachache.

"You can turn up the backlight feature on that thing," he said, pointing down to my e-reader. "Although I think they work better without food on them." I could tell he was struggling not to widen his grin even more as he lowered his perfectly-shaped index finger to point at the detritus that was still on the screen. In case I had missed the fact that it was still there. We both stared at the green blob.

The nicer he was, the madder I got. I looked back up and snapped, "Well then, you're blocking my *view*." I brushed his hand aside and picked up my device. I held it over my plate and turned it upside down so that the avocado blob smacked back onto the plate. Then I waved my napkin at him, and another chunk of fruit fell out of it, back onto my e-reader.

As it fell, I realized I had now lost my very last chance of coming out of this with any semblance of coolness. I made a mental note to search for a good psychologist later that afternoon, because I was going to need some help recovering from this lunch. I continued wishing he would get a clue and leave, but he kept standing there, looking down at me. I started to get panicky. What did he want? Why was he still here? Could we get a do-over where I didn't order anything with avocado in it? What was I supposed to do next? And why did I even care?

In the awkward silence, a cell phone started ringing. It was close by. Wait ... now my left butt cheek was vibrating. My eyes went wide, but after a split second of being very disturbed by having a vibrating butt, I realized it was my phone in my back pocket. Saved by the bell!

"Excuse me," I drawled as coolly as I could. I leaned to my right to pull my phone out of my left back pocket. "Hello?" I answered, without looking at the caller ID first.

He smiled at me and gave me a quick nod of his curly, sparkly head before turning and walking back toward the entrance of the restaurant. As I listened to a computer-generated voice tell me about my nonexistent overdue student loans, I watched him walk. Dangit if he didn't look good from that angle, too. He probably looked good from every angle.

I hung up on the spam call and lowered my head with a sigh. What was happening? This was the second time that he had flustered me—whoever he was. I vowed that if we ever met again, if I ever had another chance and he didn't run away in the opposite direction first, I would keep my cool.

ELEVEN

After my weird, messy, embarrassing, and confusing lunch (which was also delicious), I went back to the bookstore and looked for more ways to put off writing the doomed-from-the-start Bigfoot article. I should probably talk to a few more people, I reasoned. One of them needed to be this so-called expert.

I poked around the Honobia Bigfoot Festival and Conference website again for inspiration. I looked at photos of the event's founders, and some of their "experts" and previous guests. They were, uh, how could I put this nicely ... they were not my type.

I tried to picture what our local expert looked like, and I imagined this Danny Cadence weirdo fitting in quite nicely with the nerds in the photos. I took a deep breath and reminded myself not to judge. Just because I didn't find guys who were into Bigfoot attractive, didn't mean they weren't catches for someone else out there. But not me, nosirreebob. I pictured Mr. Cadence being about seventy years old, wearing thick glasses (when he remembered to wear them), sporting a big beer belly about to burst out of a plaid flannel shirt and a trucker's cap that said *I BELIEVE* perched atop his slightly oversized head.

Maybe he was also bowlegged. And wore a puffy vest. All the time. Even in the summer.

Maybe it was time to send a follow-up text to Mark, to see if he'd made any progress with contacting his buddy. Mostly because at this point, I wanted to see what the guy looked like.

Me: *Hey, have you by any chance gotten hold of Danny yet? For my article?*

Mark: *He hasn't called you?*

Me: *Was he supposed to? Does he have my number?*

Mark: *No text?*

Me: *Are we gonna keep asking each other questions?*

Aaaaaaaaand I didn't hear back again. I knew better than to make Mark any angrier than he probably already was, so I gave up on finding the expert again and decided to take another tack.

I checked my phone's contact list to make sure I had Leona Tisdale's information. I'd hoped maybe it had somehow disappeared off my phone, but her number was still there. As an act of self-care, perhaps I would continue to pretend it wasn't, for a little while longer at least.

I looked up the number for the Logan County Sheriff's Department and started to call them, but hung up when I realized I didn't know the name of the sheriff. That's right, the star reporter (okay, one of the star reporters) didn't know the sheriff's name, so sue me. Do you know *your* sheriff's name? You do? Oh.

To avoid sounding like a total idiot, I did a quick internet search to look for his name. I found it, along with a black and white photo of the man in question. It was a headshot of sorts, probably taken specifically for the Sheriff's Department website. But it was more of a hatshot, as his big cowboy hat took up much of the frame. He didn't look like I'd imagined. He appeared to be less "bubba," and a lot more "hubba." He was handsome. Maybe a little noir, even. In a law-enforcement-y kind of way. Whatever that meant. I made a mental note to check him out some other time. Not check him out like, *Hey, nice ass!* But more like, *What is your background?* Or maybe both—maybe I shouldn't rule either option out.

Once I regained my original train of thought, I called the Sheriff's Department again. It turned out he wasn't there, so I left a message asking him to call Beverley Green with the *Ledger* as soon as he got a chance.

The rest of the afternoon passed quickly, even though I didn't hear from Mark, this Danny guy, or the sheriff. Once I got home, I spent some quality time with the chickens. They had been behaving themselves nicely for the last few days, although they hadn't been giving me very many eggs. I fed and watered them, asked again politely for some breakfast ingredients, and secured their pen for the night. I remained hopeful that I would be enjoying a delicious cheese-and-spinach omelet the next morning.

I looked at the clock—it was 6:49 p.m. That was still early enough to call Bill Turner and Leona to schedule interviews for tomorrow. In this part of the country, "Prime Time TV" started an hour earlier than everywhere else in the United States. This was because out here on the prairie, we spent all the daylight hours tilling the soil and milking the cows. Then when the sun went down, we sat around by the light of our single kerosene lamp darning old socks and doing math on a school slate. All activity stopped at 8:00 p.m., including the sock darning, and we put on our flannel nightgowns and said goodnight to John Boy.

So if I hurried, I could catch Bill and maybe even Leona

before they started watching the evening's final episode of *Lawrence Welk* on PBS, or whatever it was that the good citizens of Guthrie watched to get their kicks.

I dialed Bill Turner's number.

"Turner," someone said in a gruff tone.

"Bill? Hi, this is Beverley Green, with the *Guthrie Ledger*."

"I think you have the wrong number."

"Is this Bill Turner?" I was a little confused. I checked the number I had written down.

"Nope."

Then I started to put it together—a little quicker than the person on the other end was putting it together. "Al? Is this Al Turner?"

"Yes, this is Al." He sounded confused as to how I knew.

"Al, it's Beverley. We talked yesterday about Bigfoot, remember? Hey, is Bill there? Can you put him on the phone please?" I squeezed my eyes shut and fought the urge to smack my forehead. It shouldn't be this hard to call someone's house and get them on the phone.

"Oh, right!" Al said, the light bulb finally coming on. "Yeah, hi there, missy. Sorry, forgot I wasn't at home tonight! Just a minute now." The phone made a loud *bonk* as it hit a hard surface, probably a countertop, and hopefully not someone's head. I heard Al call his cousin to the phone. I was *so* not surprised that these were the people who claimed they had seen Bigfoot.

Bill came on the line, and after some mental and verbal finagling, I arranged to meet him the next day for a quick interview. He suggested meeting at Hoboken for coffee at eight. I was surprised yet very pleased by his choice of venue. It was a date.

Next, I took a deep breath and called Leona. I always got a little nervous when I talked to Leona. The few run-ins we'd had could not exactly be characterized as friendly. Maybe they qualified as civil, but I always got the feeling that she thought I was up to no good. All the time. Regarding everything.

"Hello?" she said. An innocent enough remark; she sounded like a cute little ol' lady. But I still reminded myself to proceed with extreme caution.

"Hi, Leona, this is Beverley Green. How are you?"

"I'm fine, dear, thank you." That politeness. It was all a ruse, I was sure of it. "How are you?"

"Great, thank you for asking. Listen—"

"Did the roof get looked at yesterday? I got the bill—one hundred and fifty dollars, just to fix a little old leak that personally, I don't believe was there in the first place. Did you see them working?"

"It did have a leak, and yes, they fixed it. They told me the roof was good as new now and would hold up fine through the winter. It was a very good investment," I added, hoping I could convince her that it was money well spent. It was bargain, in fact, and a minuscule sum compared to what it could have been.

"I don't know," she said suspiciously. "We never had any roof leaks before you moved in."

A quick subject change was called for, before I got sucked into a vacuum. "Look, Leona, I'm working on an article for the paper, and I was wondering if I could talk to you about your Bigfoot sighting last Friday? It's a very important article, so of course we want to talk to you." Flattery couldn't hurt, right?

"Oh yeah? Well isn't that nice. Okay, sure. What do you want to know?"

"Could we meet tomorrow?" This was all going too smoothly. I waited for the other shoe to drop. She was no doubt holding a man's size ten boot above my head.

"I'm pretty busy tomorrow, I have a hair appointment. So, no."

Thud. The boot. Right on my head.

"Uh, okay, no problem. Can I ask you a few questions right now instead?"

"Yes, but could you make it quick? *The Bachelor* is starting in a few minutes."

I inhaled slowly. "Of course, Leona, thank you. Could you tell me what time it was when you allegedly saw whatever it was that was going through your trash?"

"Sweetie, I didn't *allegedly* see a Bigfoot. There's a few of those beasts what live around these parts. It's common knowledge to those of us from around here."

"Sure, right. So, what time did you see Bigfoot?"

"It was about 7:30 Friday morning. He knows that the trash gets picked up around eight, so he always comes before then. On Fridays."

I wrote this down. "It's interesting that he knows what day of the week it is," I observed, unwisely thinking aloud.

Leona seemed to take my comment as a criticism, and if she wasn't already on the defense, she sure as heck was now. "Well," she snapped, "he can probably tell from the position of the sun."

This made no sense, but it wasn't worth pointing out. Maybe they also migrated with the seasons, or shed their winter coats in the spring, or maybe burrowed into the mud and hibernated for the winter. I wrote a quick note to this effect so I could research it later. Or ask my Bigfoot expert. I knew I was going to regret asking Leona this next question, but I had to do it. "How do you know it was a male Bigfoot?"

"Because," she replied in a very matter-of-fact tone, "the females stay hidden with the babies. The males go out for food. Everyone knows this." I heard her roll her eyes.

I wrote a little more in my notebook. *Traditional family values. Patriarchy?*

Oh dear. I was going to need to do a lot more research. I wanted to ask Leona if she didn't think that maybe there were feminist Bigfeet (Bigfootses? What was the correct plural? Ugh, even more research) who made their menfolk stay home with the kids while *they* went out and brought home the literal and metaphorical bacon. But since she couldn't stand me as it was and she happened to be in charge of how much rent I paid at the shop, I skipped it.

"Do you have any proof that it, I mean they, I mean, um, he, raided your trash can?" I asked.

"As a matter of fact, I do," she answered quickly. "I had thrown out some of those packaged chocolate cupcakes. You know, the ones with the white squishy filling? They were expired so I didn't want 'em no more. They were still in the box, and I put them on top of the trash bags in the trash can. Then when I went out to move the can to the curb, I dumped in some more trash, some kitchen scraps y'see, and the box of cupcakes was gone! They love those cupcakes." She said this last sentence as if sharing the most juicy gossip in town.

Hardly conclusive in my mind, but then again, I was sane. "How about any footprints or anything like that?" I asked. "Tufts of fur maybe?"

"I didn't think to look at the *ground*," she said in a mocking tone, like I was an idiot.

"One last question for you." I added as much honey to my voice as I could muster for this old bat.

"Yes, what *is* it? *The Bachelor* is on now!"

"Would you know of anyone else I could talk to who might be able to give me some more information?"

"Try little Danny Cadence," she said, without hesitation. "Oh hey, dear, *The Bachelor* went to commercial, so there's one other thing I want to talk to you about now." My heartbeat sped up. I was half-curious, half-scared.

"Okay." I prepared myself for ... well, I didn't know what, but I tried to prepare anyway.

"I've been meaning to ask you. You're not raising chickens in your backyard, are you? Because a little birdie told me you might have some chickens. And chickens aren't allowed in residential neighborhoods in Guthrie. And certainly not in the backyards of my rental houses."

I tried to wrap my brain around that one. Leona was my landlady at home *and* the shop? Oh, sweet coconut cream pie, this was just great. I'd been silent a little too long and tried to think of something to say. Fast.

I laughed indignantly. "I don't know where this little birdie is getting their information, Leona, but I can assure you that I have no chickens anywhere except in my freezer."

"Okay then, dear, but I had to ask. Because I'd hate for the property management company to come by sometime and find any chickens in the backyard. Those things are dirty, nasty little beasts."

"Yes, I agree," I assured her. "Chickens—*blech!*"

"All right," she said sweetly and then hung up on me.

I immediately went to the kitchen and pulled out another Emergency Beer from the fridge. This was turning out to be one of the most stressful weeks I'd had since I'd moved here, and the evidence was right there in the door of my refrigerator. Usually it took me about a month to get through a six-pack of Emergency Beer. I'd bought some on Saturday and here it was Wednesday night and I was almost out.

I sat down to process what I'd just heard. First off, someone else had confirmed that Danny Cadence was a Bigfoot expert. He seemed to have quite a reputation, my mystery man. With each passing minute he was becoming ever more larger-than-life. I was twice as excited to meet him now, but also scared. So far he was proving to be as elusive as Bigfoot. I hoped he was better-looking. Or at least not as hairy.

Secondly, Leona was my landlady, twice over? Whaaaat? It was almost too much to deal with. This was what happened when you went through a property management company—you rarely knew who owned the house you lived in. Now it turned out that Leona was my landlady for two separate properties—and this was two places too many. Guthrie was proving to be smaller than I'd realized.

I wasn't for sure who the heck the "little birdie" was who had spilled the beans about my illegal chicken operation, but I suspected he drank a lot of beer, had trouble finding his glasses, and chirped way too much to his fellow oldsters. I was confused, though, because my neighbors Zach and Zoe had chickens. I wondered if they knew their brood was illegal? Thinking back to the many times I'd smelled pot smoke coming from their back porch (not that I would know what that smelled like, I was just guessing, mind you), even if they knew chickens were illegal, they probably didn't give a flip. Maybe I should have a chat with them to see what they thought. I made a note to research the neighborhood covenant and the city and county rules for animal husbandry. It had never occurred to me to do this before now. It was rural Oklahoma, how could chickens *not* be allowed? It should be a law that chickens were mandatory pets.

Now I needed to come up with an action plan—a chicken contingency plan. Because I, too, would hate it if I got busted by my landlady Leona.

TWELVE

Thursday morning I sat at a two-top table in Hoboken and stared at the sight in front of me. It had started with the simple idea of ordering a cappuccino to sip while interviewing Bill Turner, but ended up as a buying frenzy which included a small vegetable frittata (for protein) and a vegan chocolate donut (for reward). How was I going to eat all this? I vowed to find a way.

I had gotten to the coffee shop early because I still wasn't sleeping so great. I'd even walked from home and still arrived early. The weather had been perfect for an early morning walk. Not too windy, not too hot, not too humid. Fall was approaching and I was ready. As I nibbled my frittata I looked out the open garage door of the coffee shop, and wondered what my first winter in Guthrie might be like.

I'd already looked over the last month's sales numbers for the Book Store, and was pleased at the amount of success I was having so far. Running an independent bookstore in a small town was challenging, to say the least. Of course sales could always be better, but I was doing okay. What with online bookselling pretty much taking over the universe, owning a physical bookshop was kind of like trying to turn a profit at a

Popsicle stand in Iceland in the dead of winter. Tough, but not impossible if you knew how to market your Popsicles.

On the drive over I'd kept a sharp eye out for anyone wearing plaid pants, even though I doubted anyone would wear the same pair of trousers three days in a row. I still found myself looking at what kind of pants everyone was wearing as they came into the coffee shop. The constant looking around made me feel like I was in a mystery novel, or maybe a Bigfoot horror story. What might be lurking around the next corner?

I checked the time on my phone; it was 8:00 straight up. I wasn't sure what Bill looked like, but I didn't see anyone in the place who looked like a nut case so I assumed he was running late. Just then Seth brought me a plated peanut butter cookie. My favorite of the cookie species.

"I didn't order that," I said.

"I know. But you look like you need a cookie today."

"It shows, huh?"

"A little," he said.

I looked at all the food on the table. There was no way I could eat it all. I was about to ask for a bag for the cookie when Seth put one on the table.

"Seth, do you know Bill Turner?" I asked, hoping I could get a basic description so I'd recognize him when he came in.

Seth laughed. "Everyone knows Bill."

"*I* don't know Bill. What's he look like?"

He absently scratched the stubble on his chin. "I guess he's got white hair. I think you'll know him when you see him."

This was cryptic and vague and not helpful. "Thanks," I said, with a tinge of sarcasm as he walked away and disappeared behind the La Marzocco espresso machine.

Suddenly I felt like there was a gloomy gray raincloud hovering over my table. Ominous foreboding, or prescient weather prediction? I looked out the big picture windows—still bright and clear outside. Whatever it was, it made me lose my appetite. Temporarily, anyway.

I looked around the room again and my gaze landed on Grace from the *Ledger*, sitting alone against the wall. There was an iced latte on the table in front of her and a second one across from her, placed in front of an empty chair. It appeared that she had invited her "boyfriend" out for coffee. So cute. I hoped that one day the perfect man would materialize in that empty chair across from her, pick up the coffee, take a drink, and propose marriage. Oooh! Could this be an idea for a romance novel? I got out my notebook and started scribbling.

I didn't have time to write much before I got interrupted. I heard my name being called, and looked up to see a white-haired guy with a maniacal grin on his face waving at me. I tentatively waved back as he walked to the counter to place an order.

As much as I hated to admit it, Seth had been right. Even if Bill hadn't waved me down, I would have recognized him straightaway. Round and stocky with white hair going in all directions. And the same plaid polyester pants. It was my stalker, and he must not do laundry very often.

I could feel anger rising up from my stomach, but tried to stay calm and rational. After all, there had to be some reasonable explanation as to why he'd been tailing me, and why today he was flagging me down like I was his bestie. I reached around in my bag for my reporter's notebook while surreptitiously scoping Bill out. He gave his order to Seth in a loud voice and waved his arms around as he told some story of which I could only hear a few words, those being "blender," "armpits," and "blueberry." I did not want to know the other words. However, maybe it would be okay to give him the benefit of the doubt because on close inspection, he looked utterly harmless.

Bill sat down across from me as I was making sure my notebook was open to a fresh, doodle-free page after scooting all my food plates to one side of the table. He placed a fancy wooden plank on the table in front of him. There were two drinks on the piece of wood: a cortado and a small glass of sparkling water. My eyebrows rose in surprise; I'd pegged him as more of a Folgers kind of guy and figured he came to Hoboken for the pastries or the cute hipster girls. But his coffee selection was legit.

"Hi there, little lady!" he said brightly, arranging his complicated drink setup on the table. I could tell that Bill and Al were related—they both had the same messy, white hair and round jawline. But while Al was wiry and lean, his cousin Bill was shorter and rounder. And had a much more interesting T-shirt collection. Today's featured a screen-printed photo of Madonna, circa 1985's *Desperately Seeking Susan*. It was pulled tightly over a large round belly, distorting her face into a beauty-marked blob. It went great with the plaid pants.

"Hi, Bill, nice to officially meet you. Thanks for talking with me today," I said. I figured that was nicer than *Who do you think you are following me around town, you big ol' creep?*

"Oh, anytime! I love to talk about Bigfoot!" He pulled his chair closer to the table, not bothering to lift it off the floor very much before doing so. The sound it made was exquisite.

"You're quite the coffee aficionado," I said, gesturing toward his drink setup. I wasn't above drawing out a conversation about coffee to avoid one about Bigfoot.

"Well," said Bill as he tried to lick the crema off his mustache, "what the blazes is the point of bad coffee? I'll drink cheap beer all day long, but if I'm gonna have me a coffee, it needs to be good. None of that burnt, diabetic-coma-inducing

Starsitsplace junk." He waved his hand dismissively toward the front door. At least we had that sentiment in common.

I was about to start grilling him about why he'd been following me, but something made me look in the direction he'd waved. And there, standing right inside the door of the coffee shop, was Mr. Cute Boots. He wore faded jeans today and a dark blue T-shirt that fit just right; it hugged his torso in all the best places. He was practically glowing with cuteness. A veritable cute aura came off him, and I swore I heard angels singing. Turned out it was only Bill prattling on.

"You okay?" Bill asked. I looked at him, and his face was asking, *Are you smart enough to follow this conversation, or am I going to have to slow things down for you?*

"Huh? Oh yeah, sorry, Bill. Yes, I agree. Good coffee is of the utmost importance." My gaze wandered back to that blond-haired muse. He walked to the counter to order. His gait was smooth and confident, and I became acutely aware that my inner monologue was sounding uncomfortably similar to that of a romance novel as I watched him.

He spotted me and shot me a lopsided grin. His eyes sparkled again and my pulse quickened, like you read about in those books. This was ridiculous. Perhaps he had some sort of superpower, because it seemed my eyes couldn't look anywhere else but in his direction. *Snap out of it, woman!* my inner voice pleaded. To no avail. Absolutely no part of me was listening. We were all mesmerized by the sparkles and the sinewy muscles. He seemed to get better looking every time I saw him.

"Yup," said Bill. He must have inhaled his cortado, because when I glanced back at him, the glass was empty and he was now slurping his sparkling water as a chaser. "Third wave coffee, all the way." He burped loudly and followed it with a laugh.

Oh, right. I was sitting at a table with a guy wearing a Madonna T-shirt, interviewing him about his Sasquatch encounter. My mind made its way back to the conversation at hand, and it became confused between the visual of Bill Turner with his crema mustache and unkempt head of thinning white hair, and the words that had come out of his mouth about the subtleties of gourmet coffee. This planet never ceased to amaze me. There were some truly astounding feats of nature out there. Like bugs that look like plants, and that weird deep blue hole in the ocean floor off the coast of Belize. And Bill Turner.

"So," I said, trying to get back to the topic of the day. "You and your cousin Al saw Bigfoot last weekend, huh?" I took a sip of my cappuccino and tried not to ogle the blond guy. So far I hadn't been successful.

"That's right. We was driving home in Al's truck, and the dang thing nearly crashed right into us!" Bill eyed the food on the table.

I started writing in my notebook. Never mind that his story already contradicted his cousin's. I might as well hop on this spaceship and see what weird planet we ended up on.

"How did that happen?" I managed to sound interested.

"You know how you see those old safari movies where the Land Rover is driving through the African desert and a big ol' rhino rams right into the passenger side door? It was like that. Only in Guthrie. And we were in a Ford."

Before I could open my mouth to ask why on earth he thought Bigfoot would want to ram himself into the side of a Ford truck, I saw movement out of the corner of my eye. When I turned my head, I was once again looking at the sparkly stranger's belt buckle. Turned out he had sidled right up to our table, without me noticing.

I felt like I was in that Land Rover on safari. Quick! Where was the button to roll up the window? This rhino looked like it was getting ready to charge!

I gave up looking for the power window switch and took another sip of my drink, hoping my casualness would cover up my fear and placate the wild beast. I was pretty sure rhinos could smell fear. But my hand was shaking like a picture frame on a fireplace mantle during an Oklahoma fracking earthquake —a dead giveaway of my unsteady inner landscape.

"Hi, Bill," he said, smiling down at us. "How's your coffee?"

"Oh, perfect, Danny, it's real good. I think Seth's got the grinder dialed in just right today."

I almost spit out my coffee. Danny? *The* Danny? The man who'd been following me around town laughing at me was the guy I needed to talk to? Maybe this was just *a* Danny. But it seemed too coincidental. Oh dear.

He turned his gaze toward me. "You've got a little something..." He reached down and almost touched my face, and I was about to die of fear like a tourist in a Land Rover on a safari gone horribly awry. But instead of making contact, he handed me *yet another* napkin and pointed to the corner of his own mouth, to illustrate. "Right there," he finished.

I was freaking mortified. I was a tidy, functioning adult who didn't smell bad, and knew how to eat and drink without smearing food all over herself. Yet every time I saw this guy, something seemed to go terribly, terribly wrong. Maybe I was cursed. I made a mental note to search for *Women in 40s who are cursed to be dorks around cute guys* on the internet when I got back to the shop, to see if there was a cure. I grabbed the napkin he was holding out to me and wiped my face down like I was drying my windshield at a car wash. Seriously, what was his deal with napkins?

"Thank you," I said as daintily as I could.

I made sure for the third time that I had wiped every square inch of my face while Bill took the opportunity to be polite. "Danny, have you met Bev here?" He pointed at me.

I noticed Danny's hand was still extended, for once without a napkin in it.

"Hi," he said, reaching his hand farther out toward me.

"Daniel Cadence. Nice to finally meet you, Beverley." He smiled his sparkly smile.

"Say, can I have this egg thingie?" asked Bill.

"Unh," I said without realizing what I'd done.

I looked in Danny's eyes long enough to say that I'd done it, but not too long that I would get sidetracked by their sparkliness. I reached out my hand and we shook.

"I'm Beverley Green." I tried to sound calm and in control. In reality I was just happy I'd remembered my name. To my knowledge there was no longer any food on my face, nothing had dropped on the floor, and no piece of clothing was malfunctioning. I might be able to make it through this encounter. I watched our hands shake amicably. I watched as they got to know each other. My hand felt warm, protected, and not too overwhelmed. My hand approved. It wanted to go on a second date.

"You can call me Danny," he said slowly, also watching our hands. It finally occurred to me that he wanted his back.

"I'm gonna try a bite of this here donut," said Bill.

I let go of Danny's hand and stood up. "Okay, great." Maybe he'd forgotten that I'd been rude to him the day before. Maybe he didn't recognize me from Stacy's or our previous encounter here in Hoboken. "I understand that you're an expert on, um, Bigfoot." I said casually.

"Yeah, I guess so. I've seen a few over the years, and I seem to have acquired a fair bit of knowledge about them." He looked down at Bill, who was still seated. Bill nodded emphatically and licked his fingers.

Before I could decide whether or not I should invite him to sit down, Danny looked at me, shifted his weight from one foot to the other, and said, "Listen, I've got to get going, but it was nice to officially meet you." He smiled, nodded to Bill, swung by the counter to pick up his drink, and left. The rhino had left the building, and I hadn't had a chance to ask him for help because I was too dang flustered.

Bill watched me watch Danny walk out the door. "Nice kid, that Danny, dontcha think?" he said with real affection in his voice. "Now, where were we?" He slurped up the rest of his sparkling water, and the look in his eyes told me that he knew exactly what I had been thinking about Danny Cadence. Bill was confusing me. Perhaps he wasn't as clueless as I'd first thought. I did my best not to take his bait though.

"You were telling me how Bigfoot rammed into the side of your cousin's Ford like a rhino on safari," I said.

Bill burped again. Louder this time, and still with no apparent thought of apology. "Oh yeah, right. Yup, the darn thing charged the truck!"

"Which side?"

"What?"

"Which side of the truck did Bigfoot charge, the driver side or the passenger side?"

"My side, of course. The passenger side. If you check Al's truck, you'll see, plain as a pikestaff! There's some big ol' scratch marks on the door." He raised his arms as if to show me how humongous the scratches were.

I threw a look of impressed amazement onto my face for kicks. "So Bigfoot needs a manicure?" I wrote some words down—*long nails. Where does Sasquatch get mani/pedis?* Which led to so many more questions. I stopped writing. "What was she wearing?" Then I had the brilliant epiphany that this could be the premise for a romance novel. Albeit a super weird one. I could see the title though: *She's So Hairy.* Okay, maybe it needed a little work.

"I didn't say it was a girl Bigfoot," Bill countered.

"True. But you didn't say it was a boy Bigfoot either. Whatever it was had long nails, right? And girls have longer nails than boys, right?" I wanted to see how long we could circle in this particular eddy. "Unless they're nonbinary," I added as an afterthought, opening up a whole new door leading to Bigfoot gender identity that upon further reflection, should probably stay shut for now.

"I guess." He looked down at the ground, not seeming to know what to say next.

"Hey, did you eat my frittata and my vegan donut?" There was an empty plate in front of him and a missing plate in front of me.

"You said I could!"

"No I didn't!"

"Pretty sure you did," he said.

I watched him give my peanut butter cookie a sidelong glance and saved it in the nick of time by scrambling for the paper bag and whisking my treat to safety. This meant war.

"Back to Miss Bigfoot," I said. "What was she wearing?"

Bill looked flustered for a few seconds, but then a renewed resolve showed on his stubbly face. "She wasn't wearing anything," he said, crossing his arms and placing them neatly on the top of Madonna's head.

"So to confirm, you saw a naked female Bigfoot filing its nails on your side of the truck." Next I wanted to ask if he'd seen any Sasquatch boob action.

"Look here, missy," he said sternly, shaking a finger at me. "Is this an interview for the paper or some kinda Spanish inquisitional? I know what I saw, okay? I saw Bigfoot on Saturday night, and so did my cousin. The thing attacked our vehicle. I'm lucky to be alive and talking to you right now." He pounded his fist on the table, rattling the coffee cups and the empty plates.

"You're new around these parts, see?" he continued. "You

don't know how things are or what our history is. You don't believe me? That's your problem. Go check my cousin's truck. And then get your darn facts straight and write this up all proper, like it should be."

"Oh yeah? Well ... why have you been following me?" I demanded.

It was as if someone let all the air out of the beach ball that was Bill Turner. Metaphorically of course, because his belly looked just as round as before. But his face did seem to sag a bit. Suddenly he perked up. "You can't prove it was me!" he yelled.

I pointed to his pants. "Those are a little unusual, don't you think?"

He looked down and inspected his pants and I could see a few of his brain synapses catching on.

"If you're going to spy on someone, you should be more nondescript."

"Lots of people have pants like this. You still can't prove it was me!"

I let that line of reasoning drop, since neither of us was buying his BS. "The bigger question is why did you do it?" I leaned back in my chair and put a finger to my lips, hopefully appearing very intellectual. I stared at him. He shrugged and looked away.

Then my brain got out a crayon and connected the dots. Leona, the picketing, her constant hassling about what I sold in my store. The weird phone calls.

"You're spying for Leona, aren't you!" It wasn't rocket science, but I was proud of myself anyway. "You and your cousin Al, and that weird guy asking for beer the other day."

Bill looked like a squirrel about to get hit by a car. He took a deep breath and closed his eyes. "Nope," he said.

So he was going to play it like that. "It's okay, Bill," I said. "I'll tell her we had a nice long chat today and that you—"

"Nooo! She would kill me!"

I stared at him. Wait for it... *Three, two, one...*

"Oh."

"She thinks I'm selling stuff besides books, right? Stuff I shouldn't be selling? And she sent her minions to do her bidding?"

Silence.

"Right?" I tried again.

He looked down again. "Yes."

I shook my head. That lady! "Why does she always think I'm up to no good?" I asked, forgetting I was mad at Bill. "I'm just trying to make an honest living, you know? I'm trying to fit in here."

I waited for Bill to impart some sagely words of wisdom, but none came. Instead he burped again.

"Excuse me," he said in a quiet voice.

"Listen here, you tell her..."

He leaned forward. "Tell her what?"

I couldn't come up with anything. "Never mind."

Bill got up to leave. "It's too bad," he sighed. "Al said he thought you were real nice, and smart, too. Until you said you don't believe in Bigfoot." He gave me one of the most pitying looks I'd ever received in my life thus far before heading for the door, his as-seen-on-tv man sandals shuffling loudly across the hipster reclaimed hardwood floor.

THIRTEEN

I left Hoboken shortly after Bill. As I walked back to the Book Store, I wondered if Bill had meant "cross-examination" instead of "Spanish inquisitional." It was hard to tell for sure. It could have been a mistake, but I'd never been to court in Guthrie, so it was possible their legal system was a bit more antiquated and relied on unusual questioning procedures. At this point, nothing would surprise me about this place. I made a mental note to ask Kelly about the local court inquisitional system. It might make a great article series, once this Bigfoot junk died down.

It had been pretty rich of Bill to tell me to "check my facts" while writing a Bigfoot sighting article. The whole thing bummed me out all over again, especially when he'd accused me of being an outsider. How long would it take to fit in? Would I ever? And how long would it be before my landlady stopped thinking I was a terrible person? I asked myself the question I had been asking a lot lately. The one about why I had moved here. At the moment I couldn't come up with a good answer.

Even so, I couldn't erase the image of a Lady Sasquatch showing off her hairy high beams all over town. I'd probably have to make peace with the idea that I never would.

I took a little detour on my walk and went to the Apothecary Garden on Oklahoma Avenue. I sat on the bench in front of a bed full of different kinds of lavender—one of my favorite plants. There were still some blooms left on the plants, and they were being checked out by a few late-summer bees. I let out a long exhale.

Mrs. Karchner was in another corner of the garden, pulling weeds by the lemongrass. She raised a gloved hand in greeting. I smiled and waved back, my faith in humanity somewhat restored.

Maybe it was that small act of kindness that did it. Maybe it was the fragrant lavender. Or maybe it was the afternoon sun and the bright blue sky. Regardless of what caused it, a sense of resolve washed over me. I had a smidge of motivation now. And instead of being mad at Leona and giving up and moving away, I was more determined than ever to do what it took to win over those who weren't yet on the Beverley Bandwagon. People like Leona, Al, and Bill. What was their problem, anyway? Just because they were old enough to remember how great things used to be, didn't mean things couldn't get better now. It was like they were a gang. A gang of grumpy old-timers. The Guthrie Old-Timers, yeah! I wondered how many more were in their cadre whose crazy I hadn't run into yet. I couldn't wait to find out. Anyway, I was going to befriend those confounded GOTs, come heck or high water. Or at least not let them bother me anymore. I'd show them it was all like water off a duck's back. Okay, maybe more like a chicken's back.

Right then a fat, noisy Canadian goose flew overhead, honked twice, and dropped a poop present on the sidewalk right in front of me.

"Aw, man," I moaned. That had been close. It would have been inconvenient to work the rest of the day with goose doody on my head. In some cultures, getting hit by bird poop was good luck. In which case, Monday's Chicken Poopageddon had already guaranteed me a very charmed life indeed.

Maybe I would look up some bird idioms later. Not because it would be a good way to procrastinate or anything, but because it might come in handy for my romance novel. You never knew.

I left the garden with a renewed sense of purpose, and continued my walk back to the shop, heading toward Division Street. I continued to think of bird idioms as I went. That turned into thinking about bird metaphors and then from there, chicken salad. I hoped I had at least a granola bar or something back at the bookstore. As I passed by Craddick's Barber Shop, I spied an old truck parked a few spaces down from the entrance. It reminded me vaguely of Al's truck. I slowed my pace, pretending to window shop. Which was a lame excuse for a cover story, since the storefronts on either side of Craddick's were empty. I looked like I was loitering. Which I was.

I nonchalantly turned away from the buildings and toward the cars parked along the street, letting my eyes linger a few seconds on the old Ford Ranger truck. Yup, I was quite sure it was the one I'd seen at Al's place. I hoped I didn't look like I was trying to steal it. It was probably what people would assume, but I didn't want them to think I had such bad taste in cars.

I checked the passenger side of the truck and sure enough, there were three long scratches along the door and the front half of the side of the truck bed. The scratches were so deep they had left bare metal exposed, so it was plausible that they were new because the metal hadn't rusted yet. Hmm. Why hadn't Al mentioned the damage to me when I'd interviewed him on Tuesday? Maybe he hadn't noticed the fresh set of Shesquatch love scratches on his vehicle? Or maybe he'd been drinking before the interview and forgot. It was also possible they had nothing whatsoever to do with a Bigfoot sighting. My internal sense of logic revved its engine, peeled out, and did one big, loud, smoking donut on the asphalt of my consciousness and I gave up trying to apply reason to the situation. I continued down the street before someone decided to call the sheriff's department on me for suspicious truck ogling.

I didn't get very far, though, before I heard someone call my name. I looked back over my shoulder and there was Al, coming out of the barbershop waving at me.

"Hiya, Beverley!"

"Hi, Al. How's it, uh, going?" I had almost asked him how it was hanging but caught myself at the very last minute. It was information I didn't need to know.

"Oh, pretty good, pretty good. Say, how is the Bigfoot article coming along? Do you need my picture yet?" He had caught up with me by this point, and we stood in the street together, our hair blowing in the strong Oklahoma breeze—mine across my face, his straight up off the top of his head.

"It's going super great. I'm almost done," I lied. "And I will double-check to see if they want a picture of you," I lied again. They were tiny lies. "Oh hey, I do have another question for you, though."

"Oh yeah?" His face brightened. "Okay!"

I nodded toward his truck, a few parking spaces down from where we stood. "I noticed you have some big scratches on the side of your Ford. How did you get them?"

"I do?" He looked toward his truck. From where we stood, we could only see the driver's side. "Where?"

"On the other side," I said.

We walked to his vehicle and he went around to the passenger side. "Well would you look at that!" He seemed genuinely surprised to see the gashes. He must not look at the passenger side of his truck much.

"How did they get there?" I asked.

He folded one arm across his chest and scratched at the stubble on his chin with his free hand. "Huh, I'm not really sure," he said slowly.

"How long have they been there? Can you tell me anything about them?" I silently pleaded for him to give me another unprompted Bigfoot encounter story.

"Huh." He was still scratching at his stubble. "I guess it could have been my cousin Mildred."

Goodness, how many cousins did this guy have? I knew I was going to regret asking, but there was no way I couldn't. "How did your cousin Mildred manage to scratch up your truck?"

"She got kind of mad at me the other day. She does that a lot. And she does have sharp fingernails."

"Al, I seriously doubt a woman could scratch paint and primer off the side of your truck with her bare hands."

"You don't know Mildred!" he replied, his eyes widening with fear.

He had me there—I did not know Mildred. And I was okay with that. "It seems a little strange, in any case." I watched him for a moment, standing there staring at the side of his vehicle. Earth to Al...

"Welp," I finally said, "I gotta get going. See you later, then." I waited a few beats for him to respond, but I got nothing. I turned on my heel and walked down the street toward my store.

Interesting. He hadn't said one word about a close encounter with a Bigfoot, like his cousin Bill had sworn to. I would have thought that the driver of a truck under attack by a Shesquatch would remember the sights, sounds, and damage associated with the event. Someone was exaggerating. Or lying. Or both.

Once I was back at the shop, I checked my phone and saw that I had a message. It was the property management company who I leased my house from. Oh, great. I put the phone on speaker and pressed Play.

"Hello, Ms. Green, this is Allan from Prairie Wind Property Management. We'd like to come by and visit your home on Saturday morning for a quick inspection, as requested by the property owner. Of course, we need your permission to enter the home, but we'll be coming by at ten o'clock to speak with you. Thanks, and have a great day."

Holy Guacamole. If I declined, they'd think I had something to hide. Which I did. If I let them in, they'd see the chickens and Beryl would probably do something terrifying, like try to eat the poor guy's nose off his face. I considered my options for a few seconds and then decided to do what any sensible person would do in this situation—I promptly forgot all about it.

Before I could pick out a new task to waste some time, Kelly came in, ostensibly to pick up a book for one of her kids' English classes. But I had a feeling she was visiting so she could laugh at me for being afraid of Bigfoot.

"I met Danny Cadence," I told her.

She was browsing the reference section, and I loitered nearby. "Oh yeah? How did it go?"

It sounded like a loaded question. "What do you mean, 'how did it go?'"

"Geez, I don't know. What did you think of him?"

"I guess he's okay," I answered.

"Okay?" she repeated. "Just okay? What does that even mean?"

"I don't know—what do *you* mean?"

"The man is a god among men, Beverley. Or are you so smitten with your chickens that you didn't notice."

Oh, I had noticed all right, but I thought it would be best to keep my enthusiasm to myself. He might inspire me to write a complete twelve-book romance series, but if I said anything more than "meh" to my friend, it might also inspire a whole lot of gossip or teasing, neither of which I wanted.

"Meh," I said, with a casual wave of my hand. After I'd done it, I realized it was too much and had probably given me away. I stole a glance at her, and she had a look on her face that told me she wasn't buying it either.

"It turns out I've run into him a few times before," I continued. "Only I didn't know it was him." I thought back to the great fun that had been the Phone Dropping Fiasco and the Great Avocado Splooch Incident.

"It's a small town. You were bound to run into him at some point."

"As long as I don't literally run into him, we'll be fine." On second thought, I imagined three or four different scenarios that could be defined as "running into Danny Cadence" which didn't seem all that terrible.

"How's the article coming?" she asked, changing the subject. She sounded earnest but I knew she was anything but.

"I haven't started it yet."

"Don't you have to turn it in on Sunday?"

"There's nothing like waiting till the last minute to turn out the best quality work. I've got plenty of time to get this thing done. If I could just..."

"You have no idea what you're doing, do you." It hadn't been difficult for her to read my mind. I was so transparent I was almost see-through.

"I have a central theme picked out. I can't quite figure out the exact angle." This was the truth. All I had gotten so far was lies and crazy stories from even crazier people. But I couldn't quite figure out which was which. How was I supposed to figure out what was going on?

Kelly continued to wander through the store and spent the entire time laugh-monishing me—admonishing me for not having started writing the article yet, and laughing at me for having to write it in the first place. After a while it got to me, and when I couldn't take any more of it I told her she needed to buy something or I would kick her out. We both knew I was (mostly) kidding.

She picked out a few books for herself in addition to the book for her son, and brought everything up front to pay.

"Thank you for supporting your friendly neighborhood bookstore," I said pleasantly as I handed her the small stack of books.

"You're welcome," she said. "Although I'd like to complain to the management about crappy customer service."

Someone who I didn't recognize was browsing nearby, and his head shot up in surprise when he heard Kelly's fake complaint.

"Could you say that a little louder please?" I stage whispered to Kelly. I turned to the customer and smiled weakly as I tried to explain. "She's kidding, we're actually friends."

"I was totally kidding," said Kelly. "This place has the best service and the best book selection. And to show our appreciation, we're offering you ten percent off your purchase today."

My mouth opened to speak, but I drew a blank. I closed my mouth again. The man stared at me, waiting for confirmation of his discount. I nodded slowly. His face lit up, and he headed deeper into the store to browse.

"Just helping you grow your business," Kelly said, walking away from the register.

"I don't think I need your help, but thanks," I snapped.

"Okay, leaving now."

"I think that would be good."

"So see you later then. And good luck with Danny."

"Thanks," I said, ushering her out the door.

I didn't understand what she had said for about thirty seconds. Good luck with Danny?

Oh Danny, that sparkly, swanky, sinewy, scrumptious...

At Hoboken, I had managed to get a good look at his hands when he introduced himself. They were strong hands, with perfectly proportioned fingers. His hands said, *I have everything under control here, so don't you worry about a thing.* Thinking about it made the sun shine brighter out in the street, and I swear I heard those angels singing again. Kelly was right. He was pretty great.

Twenty minutes later, the customer Kelly had spooked came to the register and bought $150 in merchandise. I was more than happy to give him his discount, a free tote bag, and one of my most charming smiles. I made a mental note to thank Kelly next time I saw her.

Once the big spender had left, I decided, on a procrastinative whim, to change out the display in the front windows of the shop. I took down the biography books and in a burst of inspiration put up a romance display. Even with the new enticing window, no one came into the shop for the rest of the afternoon, and I ended up falling asleep at the cash wrap. This was otherwise known as a "power nap to refresh and renew the senses" by procrastinators. Yeah, that sounded way better.

During my power nap, I had a dream about Sasquatch. I awoke from it in a cold sweat. It definitely would not have been a good plot for a romance novel.

FOURTEEN

An hour after my power nap, it was close enough to closing time that I officially pronounced my workday over and done. Thank goodness I was as good at rationalizing as I was at procrastinating.

I started my walk home but somehow ended up standing in front of the *Ledger* offices. I might as well go in and see what was going on. It was the end of the day, and most likely no one was there. Most likely I was procrastinating some more.

I walked in and the entire first floor was quiet, except for the faint sound of shuffling papers coming from Mark's office right off the main hallway. I snuck by and successfully avoided detection, then meandered toward the back of the building and up the stairs to the second floor. No one was around up there either, so I paused at the bay of windows looking out over the street. I noticed the unusual shape of the windows and the beautiful molding details along the ceiling. It was a fine old building. I had looked it up once; it was built in 1891 and had been home to Guthrie's newspaper since 1894. I thought about Al Turner working up here all those years ago, and what it must have been like back in his day. I wondered if Sasquatch had ever applied for a job as a copy editor.

As I looked down onto the street, I saw Danny walking toward the building. He came right up to the front doors and I lost sight of him, but he must have come inside. Oh great. He was probably on his way to visit Mark. Why hadn't I ever seen him here before?

I couldn't face him, not after the ridiculously lame encounter earlier in the afternoon. I mentally mapped out different routes that might allow me to escape the building without being seen. But unless I wanted to set off the emergency-exit alarm back in the break room, I was going to have to walk right past Mark and Danny.

That didn't seem like an appealing option. As much as I would have loved to avoid Danny for fear of falling on my face—or worse—maybe I did need to talk to him about Bigfoot. I was going to have to eat the whole frog this time. I took a deep breath and walked down the stairs, heading straight for Mark's office. They hadn't realized I was approaching yet, but I could hear them talking.

"You never mentioned her before," Danny said.

"She's only been in town a couple of months," Mark replied quickly. "It hadn't ever come up."

"Didn't you want me to meet her?"

"Don't be ridiculous. I told you to talk to her for her upcoming article, didn't I?"

I wondered if they were talking about me. Who else could they have been talking about? Grace perhaps? I hoped they were talking about me. I decided to give myself the benefit of the doubt and assume it was me. Maybe.

"That's true," Danny sounded thoughtful. "But still."

"But still what?"

"Are you going to ask her out?"

"She's my employee, Danny."

"Cool, cool."

"But I guess I've thought about it," Mark added, as if he didn't want his friend to think he was completely counting himself out of the running.

"She sure is something, isn't she," Danny said.

What the hell did that mean?

"What the hell does that mean?" Mark asked.

"It means the lady's got some zazz," Danny replied. His voice had so much pep and emphasis on the last word, I could picture him making jazz hands as he said it.

Which got me wondering what the heck *zazz* was.

And once again Mark helped me out. "What the heck is zazz?"

Danny laughed. "She makes me laugh," he answered.

I wondered if that was because I provided comic entertainment by being a big dork every time I was around him.

"She's funny, smart, and a real knockout," he continued.

Oh. My. Goodness. Was I power-nap dreaming again, or was this for reals?

"For cryin' out loud, no one calls anyone a knockout anymore," Mark laughed at his friend.

"I'm gonna call her a knockout," Danny stated defiantly.

"She looks the same as she did in high school," Mark said, with a little hint of wistfulness in his voice. "And she's smart. A woman's got to have brains to be sexy, in my book."

"That's for sure," Danny concurred.

"But I don't care how much zazz she's got, she's still got to finish that damn Bigfoot article."

At this point, my rational brain reminded my fluttering heart that I hadn't heard either of them use my name yet, and it was still possible they were talking about someone else. My fluttering heart said, *No way! They are totally talking about me!* And my rational brain retorted with *Yes, it is probable, but I need conclusive proof.* The fluttering heart responded with,

ANDREA C. NEIL

Don't be a dumbass! Mark mentioned the Bigfoot article—how many other women around here are cute and happen to be writing Bigfoot articles? My brain admitted that was a valid point. I told both of them to shut the eff up, and in the hubbub, I forgot to be quiet, and I let out a little cough. Gosh darnit to heck and back. The voices went silent in Mark's office.

I quickly started walking toward them so it would seem like I had just come downstairs and had not in fact been eavesdropping for the last few minutes. As I passed Mark's open door, I looked in, and followed that up with a very believable fake double take. "Oh, hi guys!" I said. I gave them my best zazzy smile.

"How's the story coming, Bev?" Mark asked me, his dark eyes hooded and guarded. Not even a "Hello." He was probably nicer to his garbage man.

"Almost done," I lied. It was a lie so big it made my teeth hurt getting it out. "I need a few more facts," I added, my eyes moving from Mark to Danny, who was sitting on the edge of Mark's desk, grinning at me.

"Anything I can help with?" Danny asked.

"As a matter of fact, yes," I said, trying to sound as brainy as possible. "Could I ask you a few questions about, uh, you know, Sasquatch?" Apparently I wasn't capable of sounding very brainy.

"Sure!" He sounded very excited about this. "Right now?"

Mark stood up from behind his desk. "Okay, but it can't be here. I've got to close this place up and head out. The kids are coming over to my place tonight and I've got to get home to make dinner."

Danny's grin faded. I had an idea. "Do you have time to walk me back to my shop? We could talk on the way," I suggested. I didn't have to go back to the shop, but it seemed like a good excuse. I mean idea.

"Perfect!"

I gave Mark a little wave. "See ya, boss. And remember to poke holes in the plastic wrapping before microwaving the Lean Cuisines." I turned on my heel and Danny followed me out of the office and onto the street.

We started strolling back to my shop, neither of us seeming to be in any big hurry, but I was ready to get down to the Bigfoot questions and pulled out my phone to start recording our conversation.

"So how are you liking Guthrie so far?" he asked me.

I understood that small talk has always been an integral part of regular, everyday human interaction—I'm not a completely lost cause—yet I was so focused on the Sasquatch thing that his question took me by surprise.

"Oh." I had to give it some thought. "I guess I like it quite a bit." Most of the time. Less so lately. But he didn't have to know that part. "It's a nice place. But I don't remember the summers being so hot!"

"Yeah," he said. "Takes some getting used to."

"How long have you been living here?" I asked.

"All my life. I inherited some property from my dad, and his dad had left it to him. The Cadence family has been here for a while." He slowed down his pace so that his longer legs kept pace with my shorter ones.

"Wow," I said, thinking this through. "You must like it too, then."

"Yup. I do a fair bit of traveling throughout the year, but I always love coming home again. I wouldn't want to live anywhere else."

I wanted to ask him why the heck not, but we were almost back to my shop and it was time to talk business. I hit Record on my phone.

"You say you've seen this alleged Bigfoot thing?"

"It's not alleged. Our local Bigfoot population is the real deal. And yes, I've seen a few of them over the years."

"Here?" I meant Earth, but he probably thought I meant Guthrie.

"Yes, within the county," he confirmed.

"How about lately?"

"I was out of town for a while, and I got back about a month ago. I haven't seen any since I've been back, but there was a time a few years ago when I saw them pretty regularly, on the road between my ranch and town." He turned to look behind us, as if making sure we weren't being trailed by a Bigfoot right then.

My mind was spinning. Where did he go when he traveled? How long was he usually gone? He owned a ranch, not just a house? Did he have horses? Or chickens? What about a pool?

But instead of hitting him with a barrage of questions I simply asked, "On the road into town, is that where most of the sightings are?"

He laughed. "I have no idea where most of the sightings are. I think a lot of folks see them around, but they don't bother doing anything about it. I can only speak for myself. I live northwest of town; it's about a fifteen-minute drive to my place. I've seen them up that way on occasion."

I stopped walking, and a second later he stopped, too, and turned to face me. "You can't seriously believe in this stuff," I said.

"Of course I do," he said earnestly. A serious look came over his face. "Everyone around here does."

I shook my head and sighed. There was no way!

"Well," I said as I thought of what to do next, "is there anything you can tell me that might be relevant to this most recent spate of sightings, or that might help me write a serious article?" When I said the word "serious," I pulled my index and middle fingers down through the air and immediately hated myself for being that person who used air quotes.

"I can tell you all kinds of things," Danny replied. We continued walking toward my shop. "Usually you'll see males closer in toward town. The females tend to stay hidden. And they seem to have an uncanny way of figuring out when trash day is. They like to raid full garbage cans. You know, right before the trash truck comes."

Hmmm. This backed up Leona's story about her Bigfoot sighting. Did I now have to possibly believe these people were telling the truth? I looked at him, trying to figure out if he was pulling my leg or not. He had a big sparkly smile on his face.

I stopped again and put a hand on my hip. "Oh I see," I said. "That's all a load of hooey about the trash cans and whatnot. Okay, seriously, can you tell me *anything* useful?"

"I'm not lying!" he said, full-on laughing now, his hands rising in surrender.

"Then why are you laughing at me?" I asked.

"Oh," he said between guffaws, "you should see your face. You look terrified!"

I wasn't convinced someone being terrified was all that hilarious, but we were talking about Bigfoot after all, so I guess it was pretty hilarious. But still. Dammit.

"I so don't believe you. Nice try," I snapped at him.

"I'm serious! You've done some research, right? Sightings have been recorded ever since the town was founded. The fascination with Bigfoot is part fact, and yes, okay, maybe a little part fiction. But only part. Everyone likes to embellish, but that doesn't mean we don't still take it seriously. And believe me, people will be reading your article with a critical eye, and they'll be double-checking your facts."

Great. Before now, I was worried about how to make it a convincing article. Now I had to worry about my story being scrutinized for accuracy by the whole darn town. Did anyone bother to do this when I wrote about the fire department getting new boots? How could you even fact-check stuff on Bigfoot, anyway? I remembered Al's messy stack of papers full of facts and figures. Ugh.

Danny could tell I was lost in troubling thought. "Would it help if you saw one for yourself?"

My eyes just about popped out of their sockets and I clenched my fists. "Whaaaaaat?"

"Yeah, I could take you on a Bigfoot stakeout if you want," he said. His eyes brightened even more, if that were possible. "Maybe that's what your article needs."

I briefly considered his offer, but then I came up with one big, giant, emphatic *nope.*

"Thanks," I said politely, trying to think up a good excuse. "Sadly, I don't think there's time for that. You see, I've kind of waited until the last minute to write this thing." Yes, that sounded good. I nodded for emphasis.

"I see," he said thoughtfully. "So it's not because you're scared of them or anything like that?"

"What makes you think I'm scared of them?"

"Most people who are new to town don't know much about the local stories, and do you seem pretty jumpy when you talk about it."

"Pish!" I dismissed him with a wave. "I scoff at your local stories. I'm not scared, and I was born in Oklahoma, don't forget. But I think it's all stupid."

"Hmm." He lowered his head to look at me.

My defensiveness turned into anger. He was kind of right and we both knew it. But I wanted to yell at him that I wasn't scared. I wanted to stomp my foot and declare, *I am a local!* And I wanted to go on that stakeout to prove my bravery. I had done a darn good job surviving in New York by not showing any vulnerability, by proving I was tough. I could do it now, too.

Except part of me wanted to drop all that toughness now.

Maybe I didn't need it anymore. Maybe this time, I could try the truth instead of getting mad and defensive.

"Yeah, I mean, you know I'm from OKC, right? It's forty-five minutes away, but that should still count as local. It's not like I'm from *Tulsa* or something. But you're right about me being scared of Bigfoot. To be perfectly frank, I'm petrified. Have been since I was a little girl." I looked down at my feet. There. That wasn't so bad.

Danny laughed, and I could feel my defenses going back up. "I understand," he said with compassion in his voice. "Lots of people are scared at first. But Sasquatches are harmless for the most part."

Maybe he did understand and wasn't making fun of me. Maybe.

We walked in silence the rest of the way until we got to the door of my shop. I wondered if he was being quiet because he was disappointed that I was scared of fake monsters. "This is my stop," I said. I stood at the door, expecting him to say goodbye and walk off so I could go home.

"Could I come in for a sec?" Danny asked. "There's a book I've been looking for."

"Oh! Sure," I said, unlocking the door. Who was I to decline an opportunity for a sale? I closed the door behind us when we were inside and when I turned back around, Danny had disappeared down one of the aisles.

"Can I help you find anything?" I called out.

"Nope, I'm good," he called back.

I wondered which book he was looking for. And how could he know where it was, since I'd never seen him in the shop before? I'd remember it if I had. Maybe he had come in when Julie worked—more bad timing on my part. That seemed about right. Thanks again, Universe.

I sighed and walked behind the counter. Bigfoot angst

flooded my chest. I was going to have to start writing this infernal article pretty soon. At some point. Later.

Danny walked up to the counter with a book. It was *Faceless Killers* by Henning Mankell. The same book I was reading. Coincidence?

"What's with the name of your store?" he asked.

"You mean how did I come up with something so brilliant?"

"Sure, yes. That one."

"Funny story," I said. "I was looking around for a storefront and Kelly found this one. The price was too good to pass up, but I had to sign the lease like, right away. I hadn't had time to file any business paperwork though, so on the lease agreement where it said 'name of business' I panicked and wrote the first thing that came to mind."

He laughed. "But you could change it now, couldn't you?"

"Hmm, I guess I could! But that would take a lot of effort. Plus, I already have signage and business cards. And no one will ever be left wondering what I sell in here."

"That's a good point. Actually, it suits your personality. I like it."

"Yup, it's short and to the point. Just like me," I rambled.

He laughed again as I rang up his purchase, and we fell silent for a few beats.

"It's okay to be scared of Sasquatch, you know," he said. "Those suckers are big and menacing looking. They don't ever do much, though. They usually keep to themselves and only come out when they're good and hungry. They do love cream-filled cupcakes though."

"You have to admit, that's super weird," I said.

He shrugged and placed some cash on the counter. "I guess they like chocolate."

Danny smiled at me with those those blue pools of liquid awesomeness, and I was speechless as he placed both hands on the counter and leaned in.

"And it's all right that you're from Oklahoma City. It's also okay that you lived in New York, and it's perfectly fine if some people don't think of you as a local. Sometimes having outsider status can come in handy. Call me if you change your mind about the stakeout. I know some good places to look, and we can go anytime." He turned to leave and his narrow hips taunted me as they sidled out of the store.

I continued standing there, staring at the closed door. I thought about what he said. And then I wondered how I could call him, since I didn't have his number, and Mark didn't seem to be at all helpful.

I finished ringing up the sale for Danny's book. As I picked up the pile of money he'd left, I noticed a scrap of paper amidst the bills. His number was written on it. I placed the money in the till and the scrap of paper in my pocket. I didn't want to lose it.

I gathered my things together and prepared to leave the shop again. Now the sun was about to set and I was going to have to walk home in the dark. Which wasn't the end of the world, but sometimes I worried that I wouldn't be seen by those crazy Oklahoma drivers. Like Al Turner. And yeah, I should probably be concerned about my overall safety at night. But as I so often reminded myself, I had survived New York, so surely I could survive Guthrie.

I rounded the counter to walk to the front of the store and when I looked up, I noticed a large figure looming right outside the front door. The thing looked gigantic, and its bulk seemed to take up the entire doorway. In the murky light, I could only see the silhouette of its large personage. At least, I assumed it was a person. Did I mention it was large? And by large I mean tall and broad. And because it was tall and broad and I couldn't see its face, it also struck me as menacing. I had just been thinking about crazy people, and good lord, now it looked like one was right on my doorstep. Oh my god. Was it Bigfoot? Wait, did they wear cowboy hats? I was pretty sure I could see the outline of a cowboy hat on the monster's head.

By this point I was frozen in my tracks. I needed to figure out what to do next, and quick. Could I hit it over the head with the latest Stephen King novel? Or at least bruise its shins with it? I wasn't sure I could outrun it—whatever it was, its legs looked long.

In a flash, my fear turned to frustration. Now I was starting to think I saw Bigfeet at every turn. Had they been this close the whole time and I'd simply managed to exist in blissful ignorance up till now? Maybe I'd been lucky, having lived forty-something years in a dream world where Sasquatch didn't exist. Well, it had been a good run. I silently cursed Guthrie and made a mental note to complain about the lack of disclosure in all the tourist literature at the next town meeting.

As I was debating my next move and wishing I had learned karate, the menacing figure opened the door and walked in. Whatever it was, it had a confident and deliberate gait.

"Are you Beverley Green?" Sasquatch asked me in a smooth and very deep voice.

"Umm..." I wasn't sure what angle to take here. How should I play this? I casually placed my hand on the nearest Stephen King hardcover, conveniently located on my front display table, and began to claw at it in a way I hoped didn't look too desperate.

"I heard you were looking for me."

My knees began to buckle. How on earth had Bigfoot heard I was looking for him? Were they clairvoyant? These guys were way better connected than I thought! I wondered if they used cell phones or simply relied on their Bigfoot Collective Consciousness. He sure did have a nice voice, though.

"Umm..."

Sasquatch removed what I could now confirm was indeed a cowboy hat from his head, and stepped farther into the store. My eyes were about to pop out of my head with fear. I readied the Stephen King novel, the heaviness of the weapon giving me a smidge of comfort. But wait. Now I could see that it was not a Bigfoot at all. It was simply a very tall man.

"I'm Sheriff Branch," the very tall man said, a hint of a smile showing at one end of his mouth. I must have looked terrified.

"Oh."

"I heard you have some questions for me. For an article for the paper?"

"Oh. Oh!" The extra adrenaline in my bloodstream began to subside, and my brain started working again. "You scared me for a second there."

"You're not the first."

"Sorry," I said. "I thought you were Bigfoot." If I hadn't felt dumb before now, I sure did when I heard that phrase hang in the air like the smell of burned toast. I let go of the Stephen King tome and slouched.

"Bigfoot?" he asked, raising an eyebrow. "I take that back. You're the first."

"It's a long story," I said, and waved my hand as a dismissal of the ridiculous subject. "So anyway. Yes. I was wondering if I could ask you a few questions about Bigfoot."

He raised the other eyebrow. "Okay," he said. "Shoot."

I found this word slightly disquieting coming out of the mouth of the Logan County Sheriff but resolved to continue my faith in the law and dispense with the small talk. He didn't look like the type to engage in it anyway.

"Yes. Okay. So let's get down to it." I reached for my bag that was sitting on the display table and pulled out my reporter's notebook. "Is it true you had a few people report Bigfoot sightings last weekend?"

"Yup," he answered.

"How many?"

He was silent.

"Is there, uh, any way you can tell me who called them in?"

"Nope."

"Was it Leona Tisdale and Al Turner?" I tried again.

He shrugged his shoulders waaaay up toward his ears, then floated them back down again, as relaxed as could be.

"How often does this sort of thing happen?"

"Every few months or so. Some people call in regularly, others more sporadically. Just depends."

He started looking around my shop. I hoped he wasn't seeing anything illegal. I was getting that *police* feeling. It was the sensation I got every time I looked in my rearview mirror and saw a police car, or if I was standing in line near a law enforcement official at the grocery store. I'd always been a law-abiding citizen (ahem, for the most part), but whenever I saw a police officer I automatically felt guilty. Busted, for selling books! Oh, wait. Policeman fantasies! Mental note for romance novel idea.

"It depends?" I asked. "What does it depend on?" I watched him take in my store. I hoped he approved.

"Lots of things," he answered. He started walking down an aisle, toward the mystery section. "Full moon, tax season, election cycles..." He disappeared out of view.

I put down my notebook and rubbed my temples. This guy was turning out to be even less help than Al and Bill Turner. I had no idea what to ask next and before I could think of anything, he reappeared with a book. He placed it on the counter. It was *The Man Who Smiled* by Henning Mankell. The fourth book in the Wallander series. The series that Danny and I were both reading, only he was a few titles ahead of us. My jaw dropped.

"Something wrong?" he asked as he cocked his head at me.

"Oh! Yes. I mean no."

He frowned and pulled out his wallet. "How much?"

"On the house. Can we consider it a donation to local law enforcement?" I thought it would be a good gesture to be nice to the law. Especially after mistaking him for Bigfoot.

He smiled his hint of a smile again, shook his head, and dropped some money on the counter.

"Is that all you needed?" the sheriff asked as he picked up his new book. He glanced at the door.

"I, uh, I'm not sure. I was hoping you could provide me with a little more insight into this whole Sasquatch BS." I put his money in the cash box and prepared to leave, this time hopefully for real.

"I'm afraid I don't have much insight into that," he said. "And I'm not convinced it's all BS."

I wanted to ask him what he meant, but I had a feeling I wouldn't get an answer, even if I did. We left the shop together, and I locked the door behind us. He put his hat back on and snugged it down toward his ears.

"Thanks, Sheriff. For stopping by." I smiled and gave him a small wave before starting my journey home in the dark.

"Where are you parked?" I heard him ask behind me.

I stopped and turned to face him as I answered. "I walked to work today."

He took a step toward me. "Let me drive you home. It'll be safer. You never know."

I thought about politely declining, because something about him made me very uncomfortable—like he was sizing me up. Then again, maybe I shouldn't say no to a direct request from the sheriff.

"Are you sure?" I asked.

As he watched me, he lowered his head so that his eyes were barely visible below the brim of his hat. Oh. Yes, he was serious.

"Okay. Thank you, uh, sir."

We walked to his vehicle, a white SUV that said *SHERIFF* on both sides in big black menacing letters. I started to feel like I'd done something wrong again. He opened the passenger door for me, which was a good sign—at least he wasn't making me sit in the back like a prisoner. He got in behind the wheel and pulled out into traffic as I gave him directions to my house.

We drove a few minutes in silence, until I couldn't stand it anymore. It had become clear he wasn't going to engage me in any conversation, but since I couldn't stand the quiet, I would have to be the one to remedy it. "Do you think this is an unsafe area?" I asked. I walked to work regularly, and hadn't thought so, till now anyway.

"Nope," he answered. There was a pause, and then he continued. "You never know."

I couldn't argue with that.

I decided to take another chance. "Do you personally believe in Bigfoot? Have you ever seen one?"

I watched him as he squinted and thought about my question, the lines around his eyes deepening as he prepared an answer. I couldn't wait to hear what it would be. "I don't think I've seen one myself, no. There have been a few unexplained and unexplainable things I've witnessed during my time here, things that could perhaps be credited to the existence of Bigfoot. But I don't think I've seen one."

"Okay, but do you believe in its existence?" I needled.

"Well now, that's kind of a personal question, don't you think?" He looked at me, his expression completely unreadable.

We pulled into my driveway, and he put the SUV in park but left the engine running. My time was up.

"Thanks again for the ride, Sheriff, and thank you for your help." I got out of the vehicle, and when I looked back in at him, he touched the brim of his hat as a gesture of finality.

"Let me know if you need anything else," he said.

"I will," I said, without much conviction.

I closed the heavy door of his vehicle and watched as he backed out of the driveway and disappeared down the street. What a total bust. It was too bad he hadn't turned out to be Sasquatch—at least then I would have gotten more information for my article, even with the language barrier.

I walked into my house and threw my bag down on the living room floor. It landed with a frustrated *thud*. This was all so wonderful. It was then I noticed that the bakery bag containing my peanut butter cookie had tumbled out of my book bag. At least there was that.

FIFTEEN

I stared forlornly into the empty abyss that was the inside of my refrigerator for several minutes. I sometimes did it to decompress after a stressful day and as always, today it proved to be a suitably existential experience.

When I started to feel guilty about wasting so much electricity by keeping the door open for so long, I headed out to the backyard to put the chickens to bed. I got close to the pen and noticed the gate was open. Uh-oh!

There were no chickens to be seen anywhere. I peeked inside the coop and discovered they had put themselves to bed and were all tucked in for the night. Still, something about the whole thing was too calm. I looked closer at the scene in front of me. Ah, right. Beryl was missing.

That little hen Houdini! She had managed to unlatch the pen and make an escape. I did a quick head count, and everyone else was still there so either she hadn't invited anyone along, or no one else had thought it would be worth it to follow her out for an evening romp.

How on earth had she done it? Had she unlocked and opened a gate all by herself? Or was there some fowl play afoot?

If past performance was any guarantee of future results, I would put money on the first option.

I closed the pen and looked in all the nooks and crannies in the backyard—no sign of her. And there was no telling how long she'd been out or how far she had gotten this time.

"Beryl!" I hissed. "Beryl! Dammit!" I said it louder this time, continuing to search under the patio furniture.

I walked to the side of the house and heard a man's voice. "Hey," it said. It was my neighbor Zach. "What's up? Did you like, lose someone?"

"Yes," I said. "Well, technically I lost a chicken. Have you seen one running loose anywhere?"

I kept heading toward their fence, and now I could hear the faint sound of dub reggae playing on a tinny-sounding boom box. I could smell the ganja weed (not that I knew what that smelled like or anything. But I had read about it on the internet. For research. In college).

"Um, no," said Zach. "But you could come check if you want. The gate's open."

I doubted Beryl was so close to home, but I figured it was worth a try. Maybe my neighbors were so high that Beryl was right in front of them and they didn't realize it.

"Okay." I left my yard and went through the gate into theirs. Zach and his wife, Zoe, were sitting on portable camping chairs in the cool evening air, listening to music and partaking of the aforementioned recreational herbal substance.

"What's up?" Zoe raised a hand toward me—a hand that was offering me a little cigarette-shaped thingie.

I waved a hand at her, politely declining. "Hi," I said. "I lost one of my chickens. Beryl. Big Catalana, crazy murderous eyes. You haven't seen her, have you?"

I had spoken to my neighbors in passing a few times, mostly about chickens. But we'd never had any meaningful conversations, and I hadn't been in their backyard before. They had a larger chicken pen and coop than I did, and a large vegetable garden. "Nice backyard!" I bobbed my head with the music as I spoke.

"Thanks," said Zach. "But like, we haven't seen any loose chickens around tonight, have we, babe?" He turned to Zoe and took the joint from her.

"Nope, sorry. It's been pretty quiet back here," she said, exhaling a humongous cloud of smoke. She must have been a runner in high school to have lungs like that.

"Shoot," I said, disappointed but not surprised.

"We'll keep an eye out for you, though," she added.

"Thanks."

Zach squinted at me. "You sure you don't want any?" He extended his arm in a hopeful gesture.

"Oh gosh, I'd love to and all, but I need to get some work done tonight," I replied, which was true. "But I'd appreciate it if you could let me know if you see Beryl." I turned to leave, satisfied that my AWOL chicken was nowhere near.

"Will do," Zach whispered on an inhale.

"Oh hey," I said, thinking of one more thing. It couldn't hurt to check, right? "Can I ask you guys a quick question?"

"Sure," said Zach, finally letting out his breath.

"Do you by any chance believe in Bigfoot?"

I was a cynical and pessimistic product of my generation (or in other words, realistic). But Zach and Zoe were Millennials. Maybe they were even more pessimistic than me when it came to blood-curdling beasts. Maybe they, too, grew up learning to question everything.

Without missing a beat, Zach answered. "Oh heck yeah I do!" He said it with much more enthusiasm than I thought possible. Zoe nodded her silent agreement. So much for my "jaded youth" theory.

"Really? So have you ever, like, seen one?" I asked.

"Nope," answered Zach, sounding positively sad about it.

"But I've heard lots of people around here talk about Bigfoot, and I met someone once who saw one. And just because I haven't seen one yet doesn't mean I don't believe they exist." He swayed slightly in his chair, but not in time with the music.

It was more of an answer than I had gotten out of the sheriff in the thirty minutes we'd spent together.

"I've seen one," Zoe said casually.

Zach spun to look at her, his eyes going wide. "No way! You never told me that! For reals?"

"Yeah." She took another toke and held it in for a few beats before continuing. "About six months ago. Me and Amy were down by that pond at your dad's place. I guess I forgot about it till now."

"Shit," he mumbled. He looked at her now as if he had a newfound awe for his wife.

I hated to be a downer, but I felt compelled to check the facts. "Are you sure?"

"I think we were on mushrooms. But still, yeah. It was a Bigfoot, for sure."

"Oh, cool," I said. Right. Mushrooms. I tried not to wince with pain and frustration. I was 100% sure she hadn't seen a Bigfoot. But if someone did want to see one, taking mushrooms would be a great way to go about it.

"Okay, thanks," I sighed. "I was just wondering. Seems like he's a pretty popular mythical beast around here."

"Dude, he's not mythical, okay? Mythic maybe, but definitely not mythical." Zach sat up straighter. "He's the real deal!"

"Yeah, sure," was all I could think of to say. I wanted to debate the nuances between "mythic" and "mythical" with him, to understand what he meant exactly, but I was afraid it would take at least three hours and two bags of Doritos to get through, so I decided against it. I didn't have the time, nor enough chips.

"You all have a good night, and thanks again." I took off for my house.

I looked at my quiet coop, and I considered getting in my car and driving around to look for Beryl. But it was dark, it was late, and I had so many other things to do. As much as I hated to admit it, perhaps it was for the best if Beryl disappeared. She would no longer be around to incite her cellmates to insubordination or violence. Of course I would miss her, and I hoped against all odds that she would be okay out there, but maybe it was time to let her go. I hung my head and said a silent prayer for her safe passage to wherever she was headed. Now it was time to face the music. Article writing music.

Right after some dinner.

I tried the wasteland of the refrigerator again and came up with enough healthy ingredients to count as a quick veggie stir-fry. After inhaling my food and then thoroughly cleaning the kitchen, including the burners on the stove and under the refrigerator, I decided that the living room needed dusting.

As I cleaned, I thought about Danny's offer to take me on a Bigfoot stakeout. I thought about the sheriff's answers that had done nothing but leave me with more questions, and about my neighbor's drug-induced Sasquatch sighting. None of it made any sense. None of it coalesced into a vision or an idea for an article, or anything rational at all.

I got another Emergency Beer out of the fridge (if not this week, then when?) and watched a stupid TV show, about baking pies with nothing but household cleaning products. Or something like that. I wasn't paying attention. When it was over, I was no closer to knowing what to do.

Holy cheese on crackers. This town! It sure felt like I was the only sane human for miles around. Tonight, Guthrie was a big, lonely city full of crazy people. Wait. Maybe I was the crazy one. Oh. Perhaps it was all in how you decided to look at it. Regardless, it was still lonely.

I stared at my bookshelf, full of books not written by me. I absolutely had to start writing this article. Finally, after another Emergency Beer, I pulled out my laptop and my notebook and stared at both. I did manage to get a few paragraphs down and was deep in thought when my cell phone rang. I looked at the time before I answered. I'd been sitting there for an hour and a half.

"Hiya, Kelly," I sighed in place of a real greeting.

"That good, huh?" she said in place of a real greeting.

"Let's just say I'd rather be at the dentist's."

"Cleaning or filling?"

"Root canal."

"Hmm. Have you started yet?"

"Yeah, I have an outline." Lying about my progress was getting easier by the minute.

"So what angle are you taking?"

She sounded serious, but I knew better. I'd lost the will to care—I was now beyond trying to save any of my journalistic dignity. "You'll have to wait and see, like everyone else."

Kelly laughed. I'm glad she wasn't in front of me because I would have kicked her in the shins.

"I ran into Danny again," I said.

"Oh yeah? Not literally, I hope."

"Har-har. He kind of offered to take me on a, uh, Bigfoot stakeout."

This time she actually snorted. "You're not thinking of going, are you?"

I was silent and she laughed even louder.

Anger and frustration made my stomach tighten. "Look," I huffed. "I'm desperate here. I don't know what else to do! I need help with this thing. Never in a billion years did I think I'd be facing this kind of writer's block."

I wanted to ask her for advice, but she wasn't being very supportive so why would I ask someone like that for help? But I'd probably do the same thing if I were in her shoes.

"This wouldn't have anything to do with the fact that Danny Cadence is extremely good-looking, would it?" she asked.

The thought had crossed my mind, but I'd immediately dismissed it and focused on more rational, logical reasons why I would consider going, like facing my fears and writing a good article. Because I am one of the best rationalizers of my generation.

"Oh please, like I'd be that transparent," I scoffed.

"Okay then," she said in that tone people use when they don't believe a word you are saying.

"You need to give me more credit than that, Kelly."

"Sure, sure."

"But, um, come to think of it, can I ask you a question?"

"Of course."

"So, like, um, is Danny, you know, single?" I was fairly sure I knew the answer to this question, but it might be good to double-check.

"Why?" Kelly asked. "Is it relevant to your article?"

I exhaled loudly. "Nooooooo," I said, preparing for more mockery. "Of course not. I'm just curious. I heard him and Mark talking."

There was silence on the line now. How long would she make me wait for the answer?

Finally she put me out of my misery. "Yeah, I'm pretty sure he's single these days. He was married for a long time but lost his wife five or six years ago. Cancer, I think. I've seen him around town with girlfriends before, but not for a while now."

"Wow, that's too bad about his wife," I said. "That's got to be rough, going through something like that."

"Shit happens," Kelly said in her objective-lawyer tone. I couldn't think of a snappy comeback for that one.

"Listen," she continued, "I called to see if you wanted to come over for a barbecue on Sunday afternoon. Ben is going to fix some ribs and veggies on the grill."

"Ooh, that sounds great. I'd love to, thanks for the invite!" This meant I could take a break from my usual Sunday afternoon plan, which was to go down to OKC to have dinner with my parents. They could muddle through without me for one week.

"Want me to bring my secret recipe cheesecake?" I knew I probably only got invited because they wanted my cheesecake, but I was okay with that.

"Yes please," she said quickly. "And beer."

"Of course."

"Oh, and feel free to bring a friend," she added.

"Right." I scowled at her over the phone.

"Good luck," she said.

"I don't need luck making cheesecake."

"No, Bev, with the article. Or the stakeout. Whatever. In any case, it's a good thing we had you sign your trust documents last month. I'll take care of the chickens if Bigfoot gets you or if Mark kills you for turning in a crappy article. Yeah, either way, I'll take the chickens." She only wanted them so that her husband could barbecue them all.

"Thanks, you're a true friend," I said.

We hung up, and I flat out gave up for the night, opting for bed. As I lay there waiting for sleep, a million things raced through my mind. I hoped Beryl was okay out there, wherever she was. I thought about Danny. I wasn't entirely convinced Kelly had provided sufficient proof of his relationship status. Or maybe I was looking for excuses as to why things might not work out with him.

Why did I care one way or another? What was I wanting to "work out," anyway? I regretted asking Kelly. I thought about him losing his wife, and I felt sad. So I changed up my line of thought. I imagined writing a romance novel about the situation. I pictured a silk negligee-wearing, hot soccer mom divorcée, saving her neighbor widower from a life of loneliness and grief by bringing him cheesecakes and offering to mop his kitchen.

When I did finally get to sleep, it was a fitful sort of slumber, with dreams of Danny's face morphing into—you guessed it— Sasquatch. While Mark was yelling at me to finish writing an article about cheesecake.

SIXTEEN

Friday morning. The last day of the workweek for most folks, but not for the self-employed shop owner. Or those of us who were expert procrastinators with Sunday deadlines. I was up early again, the bright sunlight and peacefulness of the crisp morning air a welcomed change from the supreme weirdness of my dream world. I felt anxious though, and thought maybe a run would help burn off some of the nervous energy that had built up over the week. If I didn't get rid of it, it might get ugly. For Guthrie.

On my way out of the house, I stopped by the coop. The chickens seemed glad to see me, which I thought was weird until I remembered that Beryl wasn't there. It was as if they were happier without her. I still felt bad. I thought maybe I'd see her when I went on my run, and as I made my way along my regular neighborhood route, I looked for her the whole way. I almost tripped three times, but it was all to no avail. No Beryl anywhere. I hoped her end had been a swift, painless one. And if she had been taken in by someone, I wished them better luck than I'd had with her.

I took the car to work, after a quick breakfast and shower.

But instead of turning off the engine in a parking space in front of the Book Store, I somehow found myself in front of Missy's Bakery. I swear, my car had learned to drive itself there. This seemed to happen regularly when I drove to work, which was one reason I tried to walk most days.

As I waited in line to order a chocolate old-fashioned donut (or two), I looked around at the other people in the bakery. Parents with their kids, older folks with their grandkids. Hipsters with beanies. One of Mark's friends, Max, was sitting at a table with his wife and their son. He waved hello to me, and I smiled and waved back. I recognized a few other people in the shop and exchanged more smiles and hellos while I waited.

In that moment, I felt like I belonged, and I had an answer to that question of why I'd moved here. I relocated so I would feel this way—like a normal person, doing normal things with people I knew, in a small town where the pace of life was a little slower and a little sweeter, donuts notwithstanding. I felt content, right where I was. It was something I'd never experienced in Manhattan. I loved it.

I ordered my second breakfast and a coffee. Lord knew I didn't need any more caffeine today, but what the heck. The richness of the light roast brew went paired nicely with the deep chocolatey flavor of the donut. Ha! look at me, a real connoisseur!

As I stood and watched the woman behind the counter put my goodies in a bag, my warm and fuzzy *I am home* feeling suddenly turned into one of doom and gloom. I wondered if everyone else in the shop believed in Bigfoot and I was the only one who didn't. The odds were probably against me.

I collected my chocolate awesomeness and drove to the book shop where I devoured it and drank my coffee much too quickly. When my phone read ten o'clock, I unlocked the front door and proceeded to send a business-related text.

. . .

Me: *Good morning Danny, it's Beverley Green.*
   Danny: *Hey, how's it going?*

I was curious to see how chatty he would be. Was he asking me how things were going because he really wanted to know? Or was this a standard greeting type thing? How should I answer? Should I tell him I just ate a delicious donut? Or should I skip right to the point? He probably didn't care what I'd eaten. And why was I worrying about something this stupid? Oh right. That extra cup of coffee.

I hated texting someone I didn't know very well. But not as much as I hated the prospect of calling him about this particular subject.

Me: *Pretty good. You?*
   Danny: *About the same! What's up?*
   Me: *So does your offer to help me with my article still stand?*
   Danny: *Sure, what did you have in mind?*
   Me: *Are you busy tomorrow?*

And bing bang boom, plans were made to meet up at the *Ledger* building around eight the following night so he could take me on my very first official Bigfoot stakeout. And if I thought this article was stressing me out before, it turned out that was all peanuts compared to now. I made a quick list of things to consider and then spent the rest of the morning freaking out about the items on my list. Minus the doodles and a few hundred exclamation marks, my list looked like this:

·   ·   ·

BIGFOOT STAKEOUT

1. What do I wear?
2. Do I need a gun?
3. !!!DON'T FORGET BREATH MINTS!!!
4. Conversation starters? (Index cards?)
5. COFFEE
6. What if I see Bigfoot?!?!
7. First aid kit
8. Put safe deposit box key and trust documents somewhere where Kelly will find them
9. What am I thinking?

I considered calling Kelly to tell her what I was going to do, but perhaps Bigfoot stakeouts were better kept to oneself. Or was this a date? Oh my goodness. I hadn't thought about that. But when I realized it could possibly be construed as a first date, I added this concern to my list as item number ten. Then I started freaking out about that, too.

10. OH MY GOD, IS THIS A DATE?!!?
    10a. Seriously, don't forget breath mints

This might be the only time in history that a first date consisted of hiding in some bushes waiting for Sasquatch. But then again, given how weird humans were, maybe it wouldn't be the only time in history. It could still be considered weird though, and it was certainly a new one for me. I'd had some unusual first dates in my day—I had lived in New York, after all—but none of them had involved Sasquatch. I took a moment to say a silent prayer of thanks for that fact.

So how was I supposed to dress for a Bigfoot stakeout that might also be a date? No pressure here...

I did a web search for *What to wear on a Bigfoot stakeout that might also be a first date,* but didn't come up with anything usable. One result came up for "Bigfoot negligee," but I so did not want to go there.

Fortunately, I didn't have much time to worry about my list for the rest of the day, as the afternoon was quite busy, dealing with a surprise visit from a moms group and their kids. It was a nice way to end the day, and the week.

SEVENTEEN

There was nothing quite like waking up on a Saturday morning. Even on the weekends when I had to work at the bookstore, I still felt a sense of freedom and ease that wasn't there Monday through Friday. Maybe it was left over from my good ol' regular corporate life back in the Big City. Weekends were always filled with potential, and Saturday morning in particular felt extra promising.

On this Saturday morning, I woke up slowly and kept my eyes closed as I stretched. I let out a lazy yawn and then it hit me. Only, I wasn't quite sure what had hit me. I sat bolt upright in bed, eyes wide open. I looked at the time: 8:00. I'd slept in later than I usually did. I had the feeling I was forgetting something. Wasn't there something I should be worrying about right now?

Bigfoot? Yes, of course I should be worrying about Bigfoot. But something nagged at me, and I felt pretty sure I was forgetting some other thing I should be bothered about. Another important thing. Hmm.

Was I supposed to go to the bookstore early? I was having Julie work for me today, so that wasn't it. Sheesh! What could it have been? Sitting there in bed, I heard a series of soft clucks coming from the backyard. Oh. Right. The property manager was coming in two hours to make sure I didn't have any chickens.

Wait, what? Holy Flaming Cheetos!

Before I launched myself into full panic mode, I took a few deep breaths and tried to think about what the next step should be, other than relaunching into full panic mode. Maybe it should have something to do with getting up and getting dressed. Yes, that sounded good. Slowly and steadily, I climbed out of bed and looked for some clothes—something that wouldn't get ruined if it got covered in chicken poop. I'd learned my lesson the hard way.

I walked outside, and everything seemed copacetic in the coop. Of course it was! The main troublemaker had, um, flown it. I stood and felt the cool Oklahoma morning air on my face and arms; it was lovely. I could handle this. I could figure out what to do. On the inside, I was running around the yard screaming my head off about getting evicted because I hadn't known chickens weren't allowed in Guthrie. On the outside, I remained cool, calm, and confident I'd find a way to circumvent a really stupid law.

I heard dub reggae coming from Zach and Zoe's backyard again, and I smelled the herbage. They were getting an early start on their Saturday festivities. And then the light bulb went on, and I had my plan.

An hour and a half later, I was in my kitchen making myself a big giant Saturday breakfast, because heaven knew I both needed and deserved it. I was about to crack some eggs to scramble when I heard a knock on the front door.

"Door's open!" I yelled. I was reasonably sure it was Allan from Prairie Wind Property Management. It could have been Bigfoot, in which case I'd invite him to breakfast for real this time.

"Hello?" I heard a man calling out tentatively. "It's Allan from Prairie Wind Property Management!"

Man, Bigfoot was good at impersonating real estate guys.

"Come on through to the kitchen," I called back to Allan. A few seconds later a rotund, clean-shaven, tidily dressed man appeared in the doorway. He was in his mid-thirties, and his light brown hair was parted on the side and pulled across his head, like he was already practicing for when he would go bald and he'd need to do the comb-over thing.

"Hi, you must be Beverley," he said as he walked into the room. "I'm Allan." He smiled and extended his hand to me, which held his business card, and I almost laughed in his face. Every person in real estate was intent on giving everyone else in the world a business card.

I took the card. I didn't want to shake his hand, but he kept it floating in front of me until I grabbed it and flopped it around a few times. I looked at his full name on the card: Allan Higgenbotham. Yup, that sounded about right. Instead of flinging the card across the room like I was inspired to do, I discreetly tucked it in the back pocket of my jeans.

"Hi, Allan," I said in my best business owner voice. "I'm making some breakfast—eggs, bacon, and hash browns. Want some? The eggs are super fresh... I got them at the farmer's market this morning." Ha ha.

He looked at the pans on the stove longingly before answering. "Uh, no thanks. I had a Weight Watchers shake before I left the house." He closed his eyes and inhaled all the breakfasty smells, looking like he wanted to eat the air. He shook his head slightly, as if trying to bring himself back to the task at hand, which didn't involve hoovering up my food. He pushed his thick-framed glasses back up the bridge of his nose. "I can't stay long," he added with some sadness in his voice.

"Suit yourself. But if you don't mind, I'm going to eat. I'm soooo hungry!" I scooped a huge pile of food onto a plate and sat down at the kitchen table in front of an equally huge bowl of fruit. I had not been lying when I'd said I was hungry. Turned out hiding an entire brood of chickens in a short amount of time was hard work. "Have a seat," I offered.

He pulled out a chair and sat down opposite me. He had a manila folder with him, which he placed on the table and opened. He looked the contents over carefully before speaking.

"So," he began, and looked up in time to watch me put a giant forkful of fluffy scrambled eggs into my mouth. "I'm here on behalf of your landlady, Mrs. Tisdale. She wanted me to conduct an inspection of the property."

"Isn't that usually only done when someone moves in or out?"

"Typically, yes," he said, pushing up his glasses again. "But the property owner can request additional inspections, if the proper notice is given. It's all in the contract you signed. Would you like to read it?" He shuffled the papers around on the table.

"No, that's okay," I said, biting into a crispy piece of bacon. It crunched loudly and the look he gave me made me think perhaps it would be better to eat after he'd left, regardless of how hungry I was. "Inspect away, Allan."

He tried to loosen the collar of his button-down shirt before tentatively standing up. I followed his lead, standing up too. He didn't say anything while he looked intently around the room. Both of our gazes traveled to the window above the sink and out the window to the backyard, finally landing on the pristine, empty chicken coop. Keep yer cool, Beverley Green.

"Can you tell me what you're looking for?" I asked, trying to sound both innocent and interested. I knew darn well what he was looking for, natch. I was slightly petrified that he'd find what he was looking for, and evict me. That was the law-abiding, upright citizen part of me. Then there was another part of me, the rebellious, I don't give a rat's ass what people think of me part, which was growing stronger day by day. And that part of me definitely *didn't* give a rat's ass whether this squishy guy found fresh chicken poop in my yard or not.

"Let's see." He looked through his papers again as we stood at the table. "It says here that there is suspicion of avian animal husbandry on the premises." He looked around the kitchen again, as if he expected to find birds roaming around under the table, looking for crumbs maybe.

I gave him my most innocent, questioning look, and kept silent.

"Chickens," he mansplained.

I clenched one fist behind my back but put my best innocent smile on my front. "Ha!" I waved my other arm through the air like Vanna White waving at a vowel. "As you can see, Allan, the closest thing you'll find to a chicken in here is on my breakfast plate." This got no reaction from my visitor.

"Yes, I can see that," he said. "But if you don't mind, I'm going to take a quick look around."

I shrugged and smiled politely. Right then, the sound of cackling chickens floated through the open kitchen window. I froze for a second, before remembering that there were no birds in my backyard, and the noise had come from the neighbors' house. I was pretty sure my lease contract didn't allow Mr. Higgenbotham to search their place.

Allan stood up a little taller, pushed his glasses back up, and walked over to the window to peer out across the backyard.

"Is that a chicken coop?" he asked.

"Is that what that thing is?" It felt like I was letting all of womankind down by pretending to be clueless. But desperate times, right? "It was here when I moved in. I wasn't sure what it was for until now! Really, that's a chicken coop?"

He turned to look at me, his expression one of disappointment that I was trying to bullshit him.

"I've been living in New York," I added. "Manhattan. I

165

guess I'm a city girl at heart—I don't know anything about this stuff." I shrugged again. "A chicken coop. Whaddya know!"

"Yes, I do believe that's what a structure like that is used for," Allan said. He looked through the papers in his folder again. "I don't see anything here about it being on the premises when you moved in. And where are those chicken sounds coming from?"

"What? Oh, you mean those weird clucky sounds? I've been wondering that myself. Chickens! Allan, you've solved not one but two mysteries for me today. You've been such a great help." I pointed toward Zach and Zoe's house. "I think the noises are coming from next door. I thought maybe they had a lot of weird parties."

He scribbled something on a piece of paper in the folder before heading out the back door. I followed him out, trailing at a respectable distance. I'd had a few minutes before breakfast to clean out the chicken coop; hopefully it looked like it had been empty for more than a few hours. I had suggested to Zach and Zoe that they lay off their extracurricular herbal intake until later in the morning, but the animal noises from their yard were still coming in loud and clear.

"Is there something wrong with having chickens?" I added a puzzled expression and stuck my hands in my back pockets. "What's all the fuss about?"

He eyed me suspiciously, like I should know what the fuss was. "According to city bylaws, raising chickens or other domesticated farm animals is not allowed in residential neighborhoods." He sounded like he was quoting the law verbatim. I wagered he could also give me the ordinance number. Or bylaw number. Or whatever it was called. He would know. I could tell Allan knew all about this kind of stuff.

"Oh, that's very interesting. I wonder if my neighbors know that. I've never met them before, but maybe I should tell them."

"If you like, I can go over there," he suggested.

"Oh no, that's okay. I mean, it's none of our business, is it? I'll break it to them gently. I think they're elderly, if you catch my drift. Maybe a little senile. I'm sure they just don't know the rules."

"Mmm," he said.

We walked back inside, and I offered to give Allan a tour of the rest of the house. I stopped in each room, pointing out all the improvements I had made thus far, including new paint (all neutral colors, of course), some shiny new bathroom fixtures, and even a new ceiling fan in the bedroom. He seemed pleased. I explained how I did the work myself, and how I loved the natural light of the house, and how Leona was such a lovely human.

I ended our tour at the front door and when I opened it, I made a point of showing him how I'd even lubricated the lock.

"Miss Green, you appear to have kept the place in outstanding condition. I'm sure Mrs. Tisdale will be pleased."

"Oh, I do hope so," I said. I followed him out the front door. "Thank you again, Allan. And be sure to let me know if there's anything else I can do, okay? Stop by the bookstore sometime!"

He waved to me before getting into his Oldsmobile and driving away.

Crisis averted! For now. On to the next one.

EIGHTEEN

After I sent Mr. Higgenbotham on his way, I went next door to retrieve my chickens. I promised to buy Zach and Zoe some good imported beer as a thank-you for saving my butt, and they seemed to think that was fair compensation. I had to get beer for Kelly's barbecue anyway, so I made a mental note to pick up extra for my neighbors.

As soon as I walked in from the backyard and kicked off my shoes, I heard someone banging on the front door. Whoever it was sounded very insistent, which made my hair stand on end as I wondered if someone—or something—sinister was trying to get in.

I slowly crept up to the door. The knocking had stopped, but right as I was about to peek through the peephole, it started again and scared the living pork chops out of me.

"Wh—who is it?" I asked, being too afraid to get close enough to the door to use the peephole.

"It's your lawyer, you big chicken," said Kelly's voice.

"You took five years off my life," I told her as I let her in.

"You need to lighten up, you know that?"

I did know that. "What brings you by?"

Kelly walked into my living room and dumped her purse on the couch. She put her hands on her hips and looked at me from head to toe. "I'm taking you shopping."

"I hate shopping!" I whined. I knew I sounded pathetic but I was being honest.

"Me too," Kelly said.

"Then why on earth would we voluntarily do it?"

"Distraction." She looked at me again. "I'm guessing you've been obsessing about tonight, so I thought I'd help you take your mind off of things."

I'd been too busy with the chicken problem up till now to worry much. I wanted to scoff at her assumption and tell her she was so wrong, I wasn't in the least bit worried. But that would have been a big fat lie. Because now that she'd brought it up, I started to feel the angst spread across my chest.

"I don't know what I'm worried about more—wondering if this is a date, or wondering if I'll get eaten by Bigfoot."

"Sure, but the anticipation of either or both of those things is half the fun, isn't it?"

"Not really, no." We stared at each other and for a split second, I thought I might have a chance of getting out of shopping. "I could think of a thousand other things to do that would be better distractions," I added.

All she did was glare at me. It turned out to be the first, and one of the last, times I ever told Kelly I didn't want to do something she suggested.

"Fine. First let me wash off the chicken poop," I said, scowling.

"I don't want to ask," she said.

"No, you don't."

The next thing I knew I was driving south on I-35 while Kelly fiddled with her phone. She'd made me drive, so she could "work" on the way down. It was a forty-five-minute drive to the outlet mall, which I thought was a bit excessive, but she'd insisted. I had no idea why.

"What am I shopping for, exactly?" I asked.

"Inspiration," she said.

"Could you be any more vague?"

"Yes. I'm a lawyer." She continued to stare at her phone, so I queued up an album on Spotify and blasted the Red Hot Chili Peppers at her. I kept turning the volume up until she shot me a dirty look and put her phone away.

"Are you going to tell me anything about what we're doing?"

"No," she said as she looked out the passenger window.

It was a long drive.

"I'm not sure I fit," I said from inside a dressing room.

"Do I need to get you another larger size? Again?" Kelly asked from the other side of the door.

I mumbled under my breath.

"What was that?"

"I said, I'm so glad we're having this bonding time together."

She was making me try on every single pair of jeans in whatever store we were in. She'd made me go into so many shops I couldn't keep track anymore. I managed to find something wrong with everything suggested (skirts, heels, and a billion different white blouses), and she managed to put the kibosh on everything I liked (Vans, jeans, and cardigans). It's not that I had anything against her choices per se, but I couldn't see myself running from Bigfoot in heels and a pantsuit. Besides, I'd vowed to give up pantsuits when I left New York. It was comfy clothes from here on out.

"No, I don't need bigger pants," I said, exiting the dressing room with a pair of jeans and a cardigan over my arm and ignoring her disapproving look. "What I meant was, sometimes I don't feel like I fit in Guthrie, and I'm not sure I ever will."

"I wouldn't worry about it," she said, which was what she usually said to me when I worried about something. "I'm not from Guthrie either, remember? It took a while for people to warm up to me, but now everybody loves me."

I laughed until I realized she was serious.

"Of course everybody loves you," I agreed, patting her on the shoulder. Everyone did love Kelly, once they got used to her. Which admittedly did take a while. Maybe that meant there was hope for me after all; it would only take a decade or two.

"Give it time is all I'm saying," she said, trying to pull the cardigan from my hands. I yanked it back from her.

We continued to wander the store. "But if I mess up this article..." I couldn't finish the sentence. It was too scary a thought.

Kelly finished the sentence. "If you mess it up, it'll take twice as long to fit in."

I winced. I could be retired by then.

"Wait and see what happens tonight. I bet you'll figure it out."

"I don't know. I can't see any way to win this one. I can't believe I have to do this."

"Didn't you ever have to publish a book you didn't like or agree with? It's like that. Sometimes we have to do it anyway." Kelly picked up another white blouse and held it out to me. I rolled my eyes and made no move to take it from her. "Do you think I like every client I work with?"

I hadn't thought of it that way. "But you liked me, right?"

"Just take the shirt," she said, hanging it over my arm along with my cardigan and jeans.

"No!" I tried to hand the shirt back to her, but she put her hands in her pockets so I laid the shirt over her head and walked away.

"I am getting this sweater," I said, putting the jeans back on the rack.

"You haven't gotten anything else!"

"And whose fault is that? I didn't even want to come here!"

Exasperated, she fumed while I paid for my new cardigan. It was a very spiffy sweater and I was happy with my purchase, even if Kelly wasn't.

After three more stores and additional purchases of socks and a giant backpack from the outdoor store, and a new pair of sunglasses from the Shade Shack, I made Kelly buy me lunch in the food court before we headed home. I explained to her it was the least she could do after forcing me to engage in wanton consumer spending.

"So what *are* you going to wear tonight?" Kelly asked as we ate.

I took a huge bite from a delicious toasted sub sandwich and made her wait while I savored all the flavors. "Well," I finally said. "Something I can run from Bigfoot in that also looks hot."

"That narrows it down."

"At least I have this giant backpack that I can stuff full of survival food!" We looked at the shopping bag which was on the chair next to me. It was so big it looked like it had fourteen backpacks in it.

"I don't know why you bought that," Kelly said. "That thing is bigger than you are. Don't put too much in it or you won't be able to outrun him, and you'll end up Bigfoot food for sure."

My eyes went wide for a second and then I collected myself. I wasn't going to let her scare me more than she already had. Although I could totally see myself being chased by a Bigfoot and falling over because I'd stuffed too much food in my bag. I made a mental note to go easy on the stakeout snacks.

"I'll figure something out," I said, trying to keep a light tone in my voice. But it wasn't very light at all.

By the time we got back onto the highway to drive back to Guthrie, I was in a bad mood. It was later in the day than I'd realized. I was running out of time to get my giant new backpack outfitted for my survivalist trip and still make sure my hair wasn't a complete disaster. I blamed Kelly. She blamed me, saying I'd spent too much time trying on cardigans.

We hit some traffic north of Edmond, thanks to construction on I-35.

"Great," I muttered.

"Oh relax. It's not like you're going to spend hours and hours preparing for your date," Kelly said, never taking her eyes off her phone, which she'd been glued to since we left the outlet mall. Again. I turned up the Red Hot Chili Peppers. Again.

The slowdown seemed to be stemming from where the two lanes of the highway merged down to one. Getting stuck in traffic was one occasion where the New Yorker in me definitely won out. I got even more frustrated and impatient as we waited in the long line of cars that had all merged early and were now backing up for what felt like miles.

My car inched forward toward the construction zone. It was state law to merge as soon as a sign told you to, but of course there were plenty of people who ignored the rule and sped all the way up to the merge site, and at the very last second forced their way in front of everyone else who had patiently complied with the law.

I watched this happen multiple times. I didn't want to be late getting home and feel rushed while preparing for the night's activities. I got lost in frustration and Bigfoot anxiety, and before I knew it a giant white truck had stopped right next to me. It had black, mean-looking wheels and giant side view mirrors that extended out about six feet, and the whole thing appeared to be three times as tall as my reasonably-sized Subaru.

"Why do people feel compelled to drive something that big?"

Kelly looked up at the giant vehicle right outside her window. "Penis envy."

I rolled my eyes. "It was a rhetorical question."

Sure, there were people who legitimately needed vehicles that big. Maybe they worked on a ranch or did construction, or something equally as rough and rugged.

"All they're doing is proving that they're an asshat."

Kelly nodded and went back to her phone.

"You know, you should learn to disconnect from work a little more," I suggested.

"I'm playing poker."

The driver of this particular vehicle was now trying to merge right in front of me. He hadn't done it when he was supposed to, like the law said to. Nope, he had zoomed all the way to the front of the line and now expected me to let him in. It was assumed that if I didn't, he'd use his fifty-foot tall truck to turn us into a Subaru pancake. I kept as close to the car in front of me as I could without giving its driver some sort of intimate medical exam, while the truck kept on coming to my right.

"He wants to merge," said Kelly, now more interested in the truck than her poker hand.

"I know."

"So let him in!"

"Nuh-uh."

Out of the corner of my eye, I saw her reach for the suicide handle with her right hand, and the edge of her seat with her left. "You're nuts," she said.

"He can up and try his luck with someone else," I said, gripping the steering wheel till my knuckles turned white.

Maybe it was all the carbs in the sandwich. Maybe it was the fact that I was running late, or that in a mere matter of hours, I was not going to be able to outrun my fear of Bigfoot any longer. Or maybe it was simply that drivers of big giant trucks were aggressive meanies, but I kept inching forward, determined not to let this guy merge in front of me.

"Uh, Beverley?"

We crawled forward another foot.

"Let him merge! Let him merge!" Kelly screamed.

Of course that would have been the smart thing to do. But no one said I was smart.

Next thing I knew, I heard a terrible scraping sound and the car started to shudder. I looked over to my right and right beyond the terrified face of my best friend was the lower half of the truck's driver's-side door. Kelly could have reached out the open window and keyed his vehicle without even extending her arm. He was simply pushing me out of the way.

I could feel heat rising in my face, but I was riding an adrenaline-addled, sub-sandwich high, so I set my jaw and kept on driving. The giant truck of doom finally slowed, got in line behind me, and then got off at the next exit. He was probably scared I was going to stop and kick his ass. I was lucky he hadn't stopped to kick mine.

In any case, I won! I kept driving, but I was worried about what the side of my car looked like. On the other hand, if Bigfoot ended up killing me and eating me for a midnight snack, a smashed-up car would be the least of my worries.

"You are insane," Kelly said.

"Let that be a lesson to you." I kept my gaze straight ahead.

"Me? What did I do?"

"Okay, let that be a lesson to asshats driving big trucks."

"I'm no longer surprised that you don't have a boyfriend."

Kelly didn't say another word, and we didn't stop to look at the outside of my car until we got all the way to my place and pulled into the driveway.

I turned the engine off and we sat there, neither of us making a move to get out.

"What do you think?" Kelly asked.

I shrugged.

I hadn't been able to see any visible damage in my side view mirror, but I was dreading what I might find. Did I have giant Shesquatch-type fingernail scratches down the side of my car? Was I going to have to replace two doors or a few tires or wheels? We hadn't needed to stop on the way home to fix a flat, so that was a good sign. But if I had to spend thousands of dollars on body repair work, I'd have no one to blame but myself, a fact I was painfully aware of.

"On three," I said, looking at her. She nodded. "One, two, three!"

We opened the doors and I ran around to the passenger side to join Kelly, who was already checking out the car. Lo and behold, all I could see were a few minor scratches in the door bumper guard thingies. (I have a great vocabulary, but not when it comes to car parts.)

"Those can probably be buffed out," Kelly said.

"Probably," I agreed.

"Seriously though. What on earth made you do that?"

"I'm rebelling against the patriarchy?"

We stood and stared at the tiny scratches some more.

"Interesting that we both assume it was a man driving," she observed.

"Seems reasonable," I said.

We stood and looked at the car some more.

"Do you want to come in for a beer?" I offered.

"Oh gosh, look at the time, I'm late for something super important," she said, opening the back of the SUV and grabbing her shopping bags.

"Okay, so that was super fun! Thanks for making me go shopping!" I waved at her as she walked to her car, but she never turned around to look at me. "Am I still invited to your barbecue?"

That stopped her. "If you bring the cheesecake," she said. "Godspeed, Beverley Green."

I got my own bags from the trunk and walked inside, promising myself to be a nicer driver. If only everyone else would do the same.

I rebalanced my energy by having a little snack, this time opting for more protein because *hello!* Brain food. I had a little time to do some writing, so I added a few lines to my very vague article outline. Maybe it wasn't too late to start praying that the divine collective wisdom of the universe would download the whole thing right into my brain overnight, and all I'd have to do would be to wake up and let my fingers dance across the keyboard.

That was when I realized I'd started nodding off, so I took a quick catnap. It was a real possibility that I might be up all night, so it would be a good idea to be awake enough to hold a conversation with my cryptid safari guide. Or at least be coherent when Sasquatch gnawed my foot off.

Needless to say, I didn't sleep well.

I was nervous about the evening—apprehensive about going monster hunting and concerned that I could pull off looking fabulous while I did it. Or at least not look like a terrified idiot. What would it be like spending the night heaven knows where with Danny? Did I trust him?

Wait, what? Did that mean I expected him to protect me from Bigfoot, or to act like a gentleman? I kind of hoped he didn't act like a *complete* gentleman. But I also didn't want him to be so distracted by my radiant beauty that he'd be rendered useless in protecting me against Bigfoot. Such were the dilemmas of the modern woman. Hey, that could be the title of my memoir!

As evening approached, I put some provisions together for the stakeout. I grabbed my new super-sized backpack and threw in a flashlight, my reporter's notebook plus one blank notebook (you never knew when writing inspiration might hit), a few pens, and an old can of mace I'd had since 2006 when my parents had given it to me as a birthday present. Then I brewed a big pot of coffee in my Chemex and poured the hot brew in my forty-ounce thermos. Thank goodness I'd bought this new giant backpack, because I wasn't even close to being done gathering supplies. I also put in a tin of Altoids, a few protein bars, a ham sandwich, some tortilla chips, and two apples. Plus a bar of dark chocolate and a hefty stash of cookies from Trader Joe's.

If I was about to get taken out by a big furry monster, it was going to happen after dessert.

When I was packed, repacked, and otherwise ready, I added one more ham sandwich to my bulging backpack for good luck. I put on my carefully curated stakeout outfit—jeans, my newest pair of Vans, and an NYU hoodie. I officially gave up on my hair and stuffed a Husqvarna trucker hat in my bag. Then I drove over to the *Ledger* to meet my guide.

I was nervous, for so many different reasons. Neither a date nor a possible encounter with Bigfoot had ever given me cause for anxiety during all my years in New York. I was definitely losing my touch.

NINETEEN

"Toughen up, Beverley!" I muttered to myself as I parked in front of the *Ledger* building. I checked left and right; mine was the only car around. I looked over at my giant backpack and regretted not having put a flask of whiskey in it.

I began to worry I'd either gotten stood up or had the time of our meeting wrong. Right then I heard a car door close. I checked my rearview mirror, and across the street behind me, Danny was standing in front of a big, giant white truck, smiling. Oh. My. God. Was that *the* truck? The one that had tried to run me over earlier on I-35? No no no. Surely Danny wouldn't drive like that. But I never saw the driver of that white tank, so technically there was a chance it had been him. I took a deep breath, grabbed my overstuffed bag with my sweaty hand, and got out of my car.

He walked across the street to meet me. "Hi," he said in a deeper voice than I remembered.

"Hi," I said in a voice that was several octaves higher than my usual one. I tried to smile. Unsuccessfully.

"Here, let me take that." He nodded at my bag and reached

out for it. Before I could protest, he lifted it out of my hands. "Shit!" he exclaimed as he tried to steady himself.

"I came prepared," I admitted sheepishly.

"For what, Armageddon?"

"Maybe." If there was an Armageddon, it was a pretty sure bet that there would be Bigfeet involved.

"You're kind of an aggressive driver," he said as we walked across the street.

Oh dear. He was talking about the Highway Incident, I knew it! We got to the truck and I tried to see if I recognized anything about it. It did have black wheels. And it was very large. But beyond that, I couldn't be sure; it had all happened so fast.

"Why would you say that?" I asked, trying to sound as innocent as I could.

He opened the passenger door for me. "I was following you down the street just now. You took the corners pretty fast and whipped right into that spot. Were you afraid you'd be late or something?" I wasn't looking at him, but I could tell he was about to laugh at me. I looked for a good foothold along the side of the truck and hoisted myself up and in. It was like automotive mountain climbing.

"Oh. I guess so. Yeah, that's it." I figured the less I said about driving, the better.

"What do you have in this thing?" he asked as he handed my bag up to me.

"Provisions."

"We're only going out for a couple of hours," he said. "Not spending a month off the grid."

"You never know, okay? Plus I get hungry a lot."

I watched him grin as he walked around to the other side of the truck and climbed in. And off we went. He turned north onto Division Street. It felt like we took up two lanes of traffic in his gigantic vehicle, and we were high enough up that I could pretend I was in a small plane.

"Do you need clearance from air traffic control when you drive?" I asked.

Danny laughed. "It is kind of obnoxious, isn't it? I usually only use it for working around the ranch, but my other car is in the shop right now. And since we're kind of headed off-road, I thought it would be okay."

I nodded silently. "What is your other car?"

"A Land Rover."

"Oh." I was kind of disappointed we hadn't gotten to drive the Rover, as that would've been the perfect safari vehicle. Maybe next time.

We continued driving north and west, heading out of Guthrie. I hadn't been up this direction much—never had a reason to before now. "So where are we going?" I asked.

"I thought we'd drive out to my place," he answered.

I nodded silently again and I watched the scenery go by in the late-evening light. The sun was setting, and it would be gone below the horizon soon. There was a thick band of fluffy clouds above the skyline, providing plenty of reflective material for an amazing sunset. The light shone on the clouds and created a million different shades of pink, orange, yellow, and red. Oklahoma really knew how to do sunsets.

I knew that we were both admiring the scenery, but there was still some tension in the air, mostly on my side of the cab. It was like the idea of going to "his place" made me even more nervous. Those words often had certain implications. Usually having to do with something less scary, and when done right, more fun, than seeing Bigfoot. I felt like I was in high school again. Okay, maybe college. I'd been a late bloomer.

There was no music playing in the truck; only the sound of the oversized tires barreling down the road kept us company. I wasn't sure how to start talking without betraying how scared I was. But I also felt like I needed to say something to break the silence.

"I appreciate you helping me out like this." So lame.

"It's no problem at all!" he said quickly, maybe as grateful as me to have a conversation going. He sounded way too happy about going on a Bigfoot search, though. "I'm glad you took me up on my offer. This will be cool! I hope you're ready for some fun."

I looked at him, silently thinking, man, you have a weird idea of what constitutes a good time. He looked me, his eyebrows raised and a big grin displayed on his face. He looked genuinely excited. It was cute.

"Sure!" I said, trying my best to sound excited too, but I probably sounded like I did when my insurance agent asked me if I wanted to go ahead and schedule an appointment to review my coverage. If my insurance agent had been half as cute as Danny was, I probably would own a lot more policies.

While I was skeptical that the evening would qualify as fun, I only hoped that it didn't involve things like death, big sharp fangs, dismemberment, or abductions. I nodded silently again, still trying to convince myself that yeah! This was fun.

We drove for about ten minutes more, which seemed much longer since I was still struggling with how to keep the conversation going. On the western side of the sky, opposite the sunset, the almost full moon was rising, which would help illuminate the landscape as it got darker. I had no idea where I was, and now couldn't see anything along the sides of the road. I was glad it wasn't a new moon—then it would've been pitch effing black out there, and the whole ordeal would have seemed that much scarier.

Danny slowed his truck, and we turned onto a one-lane road. We passed a sign that read *Private Property* and I guessed we were on his land. He'd said he owned a ranch, but I wasn't sure how people defined "ranch" out here, so I had no idea what to expect.

We drove by a large stone house with a three-car garage on one side. I couldn't see a whole lot of details in the growing darkness, but it looked like a nice enough place. The walkway leading to the front door was illuminated by garden lights, revealing some nice landscaping in the yard and around the house. It was a modern-looking structure: clean lines, no frills, but at the same time not too austere either.

"So that was your place?" I asked as we drove back into the darkness. The paved road ended and was replaced by a gravel one.

"Yup," he said. "We're headed toward the back of the property. I think we'll have a pretty good chance of seeing something out that way."

Oh. Right. I'd almost forgotten why we were there. I was disappointed that he hadn't forgotten too, because then we could have gone out for a piece of pie and a cup of coffee or something innocent like that instead.

"Do you have a pool?" I blurted. I'd been wanting to make a friend in town who had one, so I could invite myself over during the long, steamy summer months to dive into a cool, refreshing giant water puddle. It sure would be great if he turned out to be that friend, but I didn't want to sound like I was already inviting myself over quite yet. First Bigfoot, then pool.

"Yup, there's one out back behind the house," he answered. I detected an air of wistfulness in his voice. Maybe he had built it for someone else, for a life that he no longer had due to circumstances out of his control. "Why do you ask? Want to use it sometime?" He looked at me and raised his eyebrows expectantly. He seemed a little less wistful at that point. I pictured him picturing me in my swimsuit, and I didn't mind it all that much.

"Just wondering," I replied innocently. "It looks like a nice house."

"It does the job."

The sky was almost totally black now, and the vegetation was getting denser. Trees lined the road and had grown over the top of it, creating a canopy that was probably beautiful in the daylight. But all it did now was block out any star- or moonlight. It felt like we were in a cave, or headed deep into the jungle on our Bigfoot Safari. I double-checked the window to make sure it was rolled all the way up.

"How much further?" I asked as the road turned from bumpy gravel to bumpy dirt.

"We're going to the very back of the property," he said, squinting out the windshield. He slowed the truck again and turned down an even bumpier, dirtier road. "Here we are!" he said a few minutes later as we reached the end of the road— literally and figuratively. We were in a small clearing. He put the truck in park and turned off the engine. The headlights went dark, leaving us sitting in total blackness.

I was unsure of what came next. Was this it? Were we going to sit right here all night? Was it safe? Where was the bathroom?

"Let me check my email real quick," he said, pulling out his phone. "Reception isn't very good out where we're going." The screen lit up his handsome features, and I watched him as he typed a message. "I was waiting to hear back on a piece of property," he mumbled.

As I watched him, I considered the disparity between the two major issues I had with this whole newspaper article thing. On the one hand, I didn't believe in Bigfoot. There was no way this kind of thing could exist. Humans managed to discover 150,000 different types of moths, but we didn't have conclusive evidence of the existence of a giant furry man-monster. It didn't sit right with me. On the other hand, if they *did* exist, that would be almost too terrifying to deal with.

But I couldn't have it both ways. Either I believed they existed and I was admitting I could end up seeing one, or I didn't believe in them and they were fake—in which case, I had nothing to worry about. So which was it? Was I going to approach this as a hoax or as a woman scared out of her mind that she would be ravaged in the forest by Sasquatch?

Maybe I could play both sides a little longer. Maybe I didn't have to choose quite yet. I decided to continue traveling down the middle path. I would remain very, very skeptical, while still allowing myself to be scared of monsters. Was this being indecisive? No. This was being smart.

Thankfully my circular thoughts were interrupted by Danny's smooth voice. He had finished up on his phone. "Let's go find us a Sasquatch!" he exclaimed with way too much enthusiasm.

"Okay," I said with much, much less enthusiasm.

TWENTY

Danny jumped out of the truck and came around to the passenger side, swinging his backpack gracefully across one shoulder. I'd gotten my door open but was trying to figure out how to disembark without being taken down by my own backpack in the process. I didn't see any ropes which I could use to rappel down to the ground, and I was flummoxed. Right as I was about to give up and ask for a parachute, he reached for my bag and then my hand, and guided me down to lower altitude.

"Do you really find it helpful to have that thing so high up off the ground?" I asked, pointing to the wheels.

"Oh, I don't know," he confessed. "It seemed like the thing to do. Plus, it annoys the heck out of people in traffic."

"I'll bet it does!" I exclaimed. "I don't exactly have a tiny car or anything, but when I get behind one of you truck guys, I can't see a thing."

He laughed. "I thought you would like my big, manly truck." He extended his arm, gesturing for me to take the lead as we started walking toward a barely perceptible opening in the tree line, about ten yards from the front bumper of his ManMobile.

"I always feel like men who drive big giant trucks are trying too hard to prove something, and it usually has something to do with, um, how can I put this? It has something to do with proving their manliness. But usually it ends up proving the opposite."

He laughed even harder. "Are you saying I'm trying to compensate for something? You sound like a cross between a librarian and a psychologist."

I had to laugh, too. "Thank you!" I knew he was poking fun at me, but I'd rather sound like a librarian and a psychologist than, say, a politician and a proctologist.

"I was going to ask you what you might infer about me based on my truck, but now I don't think I want to know. However, I can assure you, Miss Green, that in this particular case, the vehicle happens to be a very accurate representation of the magnificence of the owner's manliness." He had such confidence in his voice that I didn't doubt him in the least. Three seconds of thinking about it set my cheeks on fire, and I knew my face had turned a nice tomato red. Thank goodness we were walking in darkness.

We came to the edge of the tree line. The path was visible, but I'd never seen a more ominous setting in my life. It felt as if I was standing on the edge of a life-changing situation.

"There is no way I'm letting you take me into that jungle of doom," I protested, pointing into the abyss. I could tell my face had gone from red to pale white. His was still the perfect shade of cute.

"Okay." He puffed up his chest a little, rising to the occasion. He shot me another grin and walked into the trees anyway.

"Hey, wait for me!" I said a silent prayer and followed him.

We walked the narrow path, neither of us talking anymore. Was it because we were trying to be stealthy or because we didn't have anything to say to each other?

"Cold, kinda. Out here," I said. Apparently in my case, I was too unnerved to form coherent sentences. So much for meaningful conversation.

Danny looked back at me for a split second before continuing down the path. "Yeah, it cools down pretty quick this time of year when the sun goes down. Are you going to be warm enough?"

"Well..." I hesitated. If I said no, maybe we could return to the truck, drive back to Guthrie, and warm up with a veggie deluxe at the Pizza Palace. "I'll be fine."

"You don't sound so sure," he said without turning around.

"Just show me the Sasquatch," I snapped. "And that's not a euphemism," I mumbled to myself.

"Pardon?"

"Nothing."

"Don't worry, we're almost there."

I hoped so, although I wasn't sure where "there" was. Meanwhile, I tried to banish visions of being dragged off into the wilderness by a Bigfoot and dying of hypothermia. As long as I didn't get separated from my snacks, I would be okay.

After walking for what seemed like days, we came to a small clearing, at the edge of which stood a small cabin. It was a simple wooden structure—nothing fancy, but not quite a shack either.

A narrow porch that ran along the front, with a bench placed under one large window. It looked inviting, in a non-Bigfoot-hideout kind of way. Danny got to the door and unlocked it, waiting for me to catch up. I was about to walk in when he leaned over and stretched his arm out in front of me. I held my breath in anticipation as he continued to reach... and flipped on a light switch right inside the door. He noticed my raised eyebrows as he invaded my personal space.

"Pardon me," he said, stifling a laugh.

I shot him a look and walked in. It was the most action I'd seen in almost a year, but he didn't have to know that.

"Kind of touchy today, huh? Oh wait, you're that way every time I see you."

The overhead light cast a harsh glare over the room, and my eyes were having trouble adjusting. I was about to launch into an angry speech about how stupid that was, I was not touchy, thank you very much. But for once I thought before I spoke and realized he was right. Whether I had food on my face, or had dropped my coffee, or was about to be dinner for Bigfoot, he seemed to catch me when I was most perturbed. And he may have even caught me when I was being a jerk on the freeway. Why would this nice person want to spend any time with me at all, if I was always such a beyatch?

"Sorry, I'm a little on edge," I admitted. I tried to soften the features of my face, which felt permanently stuck in serious stress mode. "At least tonight anyway, it's the whole 'I'm mortally terrified of Bigfoot' thing. I'll try to be more, um, jovial. I promise."

"It's okay," Danny said calmly as he closed and locked the door. "I haven't known you for long, but I feel like 'jovial' might be a stretch." He poised his hand over the light switch on the wall. "Can you turn that on?" he asked, nodding toward a small reading lamp by a large comfy chair.

I did as he asked, and he flipped the overhead light off. "You might be right. In any case, sorry."

"I understand. But don't worry, okay? You're safe here with me."

I could feel my facial features start to sharpen again, but tried to stop, as promised. *Jovial?* Yeah, probably not. I hoped he was right about being safe though. I might be able to trust Danny, but I wasn't so sure about Bigfoot.

The room was much darker now, lit only by one small, warm light. I took a look around at our surroundings; we had entered into a large space that served as a kitchen, eating area, and living room. From what I could tell, there was maybe one bedroom and a bathroom down a short hallway in the back, and that was it. The walls and floor were bare wood, and there were two oversized chairs and a small coffee table arranged around a fireplace on the wall opposite the kitchen. It looked cozy. Like, it would have been a nice place to stay while doing anything other than what we were actually there for.

"These are fancy digs for a stakeout," I said.

"We could have used the hunting stand out by the lake, but I thought you might be a little more comfortable here, since it's cold tonight. We'll be able to see fine from that window, if this goes like I think it will." He pointed to the big picture window that was covered by some simple gray drapes.

Yup, it was nice and warm and cozy. A girl could get to feeling romantic in a place like this. And then I remembered why we were there.

I looked closely at the door to make sure it was securely locked. It was, and it appeared that all I had to do was flip the deadbolt to get out if I needed to escape quickly. I didn't know Danny, and here I was placing my life in his hands. Would there be more threat from outside the cabin or from inside? Was Danny more dangerous than Bigfoot?

All the scary Bigfoot scenarios my sister had teased me with way back when came rushing back. Bigfoot was going to make me cook him breakfast in that kitchen over there. I cursed my sister Emily under my breath.

I had to remember that Danny was best friends with Mark, and even Kelly had vouched for him. But I still hoped the GPS was working on my phone, in case this turned out to be a cabin of death and I got trapped and someone would need to come look for my carcass.

I sat down in one of the comfy chairs, noting that it felt as comfy as it looked. My eye caught sight of two rifles next to the door in a wall-mounted gun rack. He saw me looking at them.

"This place gets used for hunting trips sometimes, or as a guest house. It hasn't been used much lately, but I had it prepared for tonight." He bent down and lit two pillar candles on the coffee table. They made a nice warm light. Romantic almost. Almost.

"Prepared how?" I asked, watching the flickering candle flames. Did that mean clean sheets on the bed, or a fresh can of Pringles in the pantry? Or both? The candles seemed overkill for a hunting shack.

"Oh, I had it cleaned today. It gets pretty dusty in here, especially when it sits empty for a while." He walked to the kitchen and checked the pantry. "And I had some snacks brought over. I know how you like to eat." His shoulders hunched up a little, like he was expecting me to throw something at him. I had thought about it but didn't have anything handy.

Just then we heard a sound from outside the cabin. It wasn't very loud, but it was a distinct rustling sound. I froze, and Danny stood up a little taller, listening intently.

"What was that?" I whispered. "What do we do?" I eyed the guns on the wall as my stomach tensed up.

We heard the noise again, and Danny looked at his watch before slowly making his way to the window. He pulled the heavy curtain aside a few inches and peered out at the clearing. "It's nothing," he said. "Raccoon." He sat back down in the other chair.

"How will we know if Bigfoot is out there if we're sitting here relaxing by candlelight?" I asked. "Will he knock on the door to let us know he's stopping by?"

Danny shot me an exasperated look. "Clearly you haven't been hunting before," he said.

I crossed my arms over my chest. "What gave it away?"

He went to the kitchen again, picked up a small laptop from the counter, and brought it back to his chair. He opened it and began fiddling with it for a minute or two. "Here we go!" he exclaimed. He put it on the coffee table in front of me and moved his chair closer to mine. "Look," he said, pointing to the screen. It displayed a grainy black-and-white video feed of a small clearing surrounded by trees.

"Is this a new series on Netflix?" I had no idea what I was looking at.

"It's what's going on right outside the front door," he said as if talking to a small child. "We listen for different sounds and keep an eye on this." He leaned back in his chair. "Now, I think we need something to drink, don't you?" He eyed my backpack.

"What makes you think I brought something to drink?" I asked.

He eyed my backpack. Enough said.

I rifled through my bag and pulled out the thermos of coffee. I poured some into two mugs Danny had brought from the kitchen, and we sat drinking the hot, strong brew.

"This is so good," he said as he smelled the steam coming off the top of his second cup. "But I'd expect nothing less. I've heard you're a real connoisseur."

"From who?"

"Seth told me." He smiled.

I guess Mark hadn't been the only person he'd asked about me. That was a good sign, right?

"Yes, I know a little bit about coffee. It's all about quality, not quantity," I said. "So how long have you known Bill?"

"Who says I know Bill?"

"You came up to him and said hello in Hoboken the other day? While I was there?" I reminded him.

"Oh, right. I guess you live here long enough, and you get to know all the Turners."

"How many of them are there?"

"Enough to start a pro football team."

"Hmm," I said absently.

"Why?"

I leaned forward in my chair. "I think he was following me last week. It was creepy, you know? How do I know he's not some stalker weirdo?"

Danny laughed at that. "Oh man, that's funny. Bill is the most harmless person you'll ever meet." He was silent for a few beats. "Maybe it has something to do with your store? I remember hearing something about Leona and them wanting to shut you down."

"Yeah, I guess so. My landlady is a real piece of work." I rolled my eyes. "Wait, how do you know about all that?"

"It's a small town and word travels fast. Especially when it has to do with scandal."

I could feel my face reddening. "There *is* no scandal!"

"I know that, and you know that, but clearly your landlady doesn't."

"Ugh, Leona." I leaned back again and made a dramatic *thud* against the chair.

"I'd like to say she was as harmless as Bill." I looked at him and he shrugged. "Oh well. Just keep up all your hard work. This town needs your bookstore, and needs someone like you." He flashed that smile at me again, and I felt much better.

"Thanks," I said. "I'll try."

I got up from my chair and walked to the window. I wanted to look outside, but not really.

"Does Bigfoot know how to use power tools?" I asked.

Danny stopped with his cup halfway to his mouth. "Excuse me?"

"Does Bigfoot know how to use power tools," I repeated. "Or how about gardening equipment. Shovels? Axes? Large kitchen spoons?" How sophisticated was Bigfoot? I wanted to know what we were up against.

"You know, I'm not sure. As far as I know, they only use their hands to—"

Nope nope nope, didn't want to hear the end of that sentence. So I cut him off. "How can you be sure we'll see one tonight?"

"I put some snacks out in that clearing," he said.

"That clearing right out there?" I jerked my thumb toward the door.

"Yup."

"Right outside this door."

"Right out there." He was enjoying this.

"What kind of snacks?"

"Hostess Cupcakes. They love those things. Don't ask me how I know."

"Okay," I answered. I hadn't planned on asking.

"Don't worry, I'm not part Sasquatch," he chided. "You can check my birth certificate."

I smiled. He got up and walked to the window to stand next to me and reached out to move the curtain aside. He was so close I could detect a faint whiff of clean soap smell. My breath caught in my throat. He smelled so manly. And clean.

"It's okay," he said softly as he peered outside. "I'll protect you." He turned to look at me, and we were so close that when I looked into his blue eyes, I almost fell into them. I needed to get off my feet before I started swooning, so I sat back down and checked the video feed from the clearing. Nothing.

He sat back down, too, and we made quiet small talk for a while, sometimes stopping to listen to a noise coming from outside. They were all false alarms, but I jumped every time. Finally, he reached into his bag and pulled out a flask and offered it to me. I gladly accepted. Great minds think alike; greater minds remember to pack the flask.

I took a sip; whatever it was tasted smooth going down at first, but then made my esophagus catch on fire, and I started coughing.

"Nice," I said in a hoarse whisper. Clearly I wasn't much for imbibing the hard stuff. I passed the flask back.

"So," he said, "Be-ver-ley." He pronounced each syllable slowly.

"Dan-ny."

"Your name."

"What about it?"

"It's kind of old-fashioned, isn't it? I mean, you're not actually eighty or something, are you?" He took a swig from the flask before passing it back to me.

"What can I say," I sighed. "My parents are old-fashioned. They still think their 1982 touch-tone house phone is a technological miracle."

He laughed. I couldn't tell if he thought I was that funny or if he'd been hitting the flask a little harder than I was.

"It's a family name," I continued. "I was named after my maternal grandmother. I know it's dated. Heck, it's downright old. But it's me." I shrugged and took another swig and only coughed once. "And I loved that old broad," I added. Good old MeeMo.

"Well, I like it," he decided.

"What, this hooch?" I held up the flask. Maybe I should slow down a little, too.

"Hooch? No, your name." He stood up and went to the window one more time.

I rifled through my two-ton backpack, this time pulling out a ham sandwich. I should probably put some actual food in my stomach with all that alcohol. I held it out half of the sandwich to Danny. "You want?"

He walked back to take it, then sat down heavily in his chair. "Thanks," he said and started eating. "This is delicious!

Seriously, this is so good." He inhaled the rest. "What's on this?"

"The number one key to happiness in life," I confided to him with my mouth full of sandwich, "is to never *ever* skimp on the mayo."

"You've made me a believer," he said happily, brushing a few crumbs off his shirt. Right then I knew that this man was true relationship material. I could never love a man who didn't love mayo.

Apparently, it was his turn to share again because he leaned over and pulled something out of his bag and tossed it to me. A package of Hostess Cupcakes. "No sense in Sasquatch getting all the good snacks." We both started laughing as we pulled the crinkly plastic covers apart to eat the squishy plastic cupcakes inside.

Another hour went by, and we spent it snacking, checking the window, and getting to know each other better. Except for the fact that I was locked in a small cabin with one man and a few guns and we were trying to get a glimpse of a scary monster on purpose, it was a pleasant enough way to spend an evening. I'd had worse times with a guy.

Maybe it was the contents of the flask; maybe it was how easy it was to talk to Danny. Or perhaps it was the candlelight, but I seemed to go for longer stretches of time without feeling scared. There was still the distinct possibility that if there was a long enough lull in the conversation, we might hear Bigfoot mouth-breathing right outside the door, but I was starting to enjoy myself more. Danny was funny, smart, and open, and he made me laugh. Dare I say, I was having a good time.

Suddenly, we heard a commotion outside. It sounded like water splashing followed by gravel being run through a garbage disposal. We looked at each other, and got up from our chairs to sneak over to the window. Danny pulled the curtain back ever so slightly, and we looked out together. We stood so close that our shirtsleeves were touching. For a split second I felt a spark igniting between us. Fabric on fabric, baby! I imagined our shirts falling in love and running off to Martinique together.

"Right there, do you see?" he whispered excitedly.

I couldn't see much of anything.

"There, by that oak tree!"

"Oh, I think so!" I said, still not knowing what I was supposed to be looking at. I was terrified and excited, and also feeling very attracted to Danny. It had been there all along, but only under the influence of alcohol, cupcakes, and the threat of death could I fully admit it to myself. I tried to refocus and look even harder out the window. "Oh!" I scream-whispered.

I saw something creeping along the tree line. It appeared to be a big, black, and possibly furry blob. The blob stopped to pick something up off the ground, held it up to its face, and looked left and right like it was about to cross a street. Then it disappeared back into the trees. I started breathing again. We stood there for a few seconds, not saying anything, not moving. I was elated, confused, and scared. Standing so close to Danny combined with what I'd just seen was all too overwhelming.

I turned to him, and before I knew what was happening, he kissed me.

His lips were soft, and they knew what they were doing and where they were supposed to go. I considered pulling back, but my girlie parts threatened my brain with an all-out revolt, and my brain wisely acquiesced.

The kiss lasted for an hour, and I heard angels singing to harp music, and the clouds parted and rays of golden sunshine streamed through the room. At least it seemed like an hour. And I do think I heard harp music coming from somewhere. But in reality, our kiss was brief. He pulled away from me slowly, kissing me once on the side of my neck before leaning back to look at me. His eyes were soft, and his lips were still parted.

"What in the great heavens above was that?" I asked as Danny let the curtain drop back in front of the window.

"First base?"

"No. I mean, yes. Wait. No, the thing outside." The speech part of my brain was not yet working properly.

"Oh, that. I'll give you three guesses," he said. "Come here." He led me to the chairs and motioned for me to sit down. He picked up the laptop and sat on the arm of my chair, placing the computer in my lap. "Let's take a look-see."

He leaned in to run the video back a few minutes and hit play. I could hear him breathing, and suddenly my heartbeat became very loud in my ears and I thought I might pass out. Was Danny more scary than seeing Bigfoot? Was that really even Bigfoot? Was he still out there? Why was Danny scary? His lips certainly weren't scary.

"Here we go," he mumbled, pointing to a spot on the screen. We watched the blob reach down to the ground and then take off running.

"I'm not sure what I'm looking at," I said, as a true reporter would.

He turned his head toward me, his eyes bright in the dim room. "I would think it's obvious."

"Not in the least! I couldn't tell if that was Bigfoot or Bob Hope."

"Bob Hope is dead. And Bigfoot wasn't wearing golf shoes."

"They *say* Bob Hope is dead, but they also say there is no such thing as Bigfoot."

"Yes but we've got one on video, and you saw it for yourself, right out there," Danny said.

One side of my mouth slid upward as I tried to look skeptical. I was still taking the middle road—slightly terrified but doubtful as all get-out. I had seen something, but it could have been anything. It could have been the same giant meatloaf that Al Turner had described. I wasn't going to admit anything.

"Maybe we need to get one of those Bigfoot experts down in Honobia to verify this for us," I suggested, pointing to the laptop.

"Oh come on, those wahoos wouldn't know a Sasquatch from a hole in the ground. I'm telling you, we saw Bigfoot tonight!" He closed the computer and folded his arms in front of his chest, satisfied that our work was done.

"Okay, if you say so." I yawned. I already knew those Honobia experts were wahoos—everyone was. I suddenly felt very sleepy. It was close to two in the morning. The day had finally caught up with me, and agreeing with Danny seemed like the easiest path to take. I thought about that kiss though. Who cared about Sasquatch after a kiss like that? What did it mean exactly? Let the second-guessing begin!

I needed to go home and get some sleep. When it came to a possible romance, I didn't want to get carried away and make the same mistakes I'd kept making in New York. I wanted to be smart this time, and I knew that things had to be handled differently in a small town. It was only a kiss, after all.

Danny watched me yawn again. "Let's get you home and into bed," he said. "I mean, you know, your bed. Your home, with like, I mean ... Yeah."

I laughed. "I know what you mean. Yes, let's head out. I think I've seen enough."

TWENTY-ONE

We packed up our bags and Danny blew out the candles and tidied up the kitchen. As we went to leave, he pulled a rifle off the wall and checked the safety before placing it under his arm.

"What do you need that for?" I asked.

"We saw a Bigfoot out there. He could still be around." He opened the door and ushered me outside.

I stopped in my tracks, half in the cabin, half out. "What the what?" I hadn't thought of this. That thing could be *right out there*.

"Don't worry," Danny assured me. "He just had a snack. He's happy, and probably took half of it back to his wife. I mean domestic partner. Anyway, he's long gone by now. At least, I'm reasonably sure."

I eyed the rifle under his arm. "I'm only bringing this with us to make you feel better," he explained.

"Riiiiiight," I drawled.

He finally managed to get me out the door and locked up the cabin behind us. As we walked back to his truck, I noticed the moon was even lower on the horizon now, and soon it would be completely obscured by trees.

We trudged along the path, both of us pretty tired by this point. I replayed the surprise kiss in my mind. I definitely hadn't seen that coming, although I certainly didn't mind that it had. Thank goodness I'd brought those breath mints.

But what had it meant? Ugh. Of course I would go straight to *What does it mean* rather than simply enjoy the niceness of what it had been. Perhaps it was a trait of the female gender to wonder what everything *meant,* while dudes simply moved on to the next piece of business, whatever it was. I knew how it worked when it came to romance novels, but not when it came to real life.

I watched Danny lead the way in front of me, his boots crunching the dirt as we walked along the path. He had a light jacket on, his backpack was slung over his left shoulder, and he held the gun tucked under his right arm. I enjoyed observing the sway of his hips as he walked. Aw, to heck with where it was headed. It had been a great kiss. And I wouldn't mind more.

My stomach growled, and it pulled me out of my reverie. Even though we had snacked plenty, I hadn't eaten anything with much substance over the course of the evening. I stuck my hand into the outside pocket of my backpack and pulled out a package containing two Hostess Cupcakes that Danny must have stuck in there before we left. It was easier than searching through the whole bag for something healthier.

"So how do you feel after having seen your first Bigfoot?" Danny asked, turning his head to the side so I could hear him talk.

"Hmm. I guess I feel suspicious," I said with a mouthful of cupcake.

He stopped in his tracks. "What do you mean?"

I waited till I had finished my mouthful of dessert to continue. "It was all too easy," I observed, as I caught up to him on the trail. "We tossed a cupcake out the door, waited a few hours, and presto, a Bigfoot?"

"I—that's ridiculous! You saw it with your own eyes. That wasn't fake!"

"I saw a dark blob across a big clearing. And I saw a grainy dark blob in some grainy dark video footage. Proves nothing." I hoped.

He looked downright dejected now, and I felt bad. "Don't get me wrong," I continued. "I'm very grateful that you took time to bring me out here, honest! You're very knowledgeable about Bigfoot, and I have plenty of material for my article now. And I had a really nice time." I thought about that kiss again. "But I'm not quite ready to admit I saw a Bigfoot. Sorry." I shrugged and continued up the path.

I heard Danny's footsteps start back up behind me, but then suddenly stop again. I turned to face him. He had a strange look on his face.

"What?" I asked.

He looked down at his feet. "Okay, I can't lie to you. I thought it would be fun, but I guess I can't go through with it. You're right. That wasn't a Bigfoot."

"Aha! I knew it! Vindication! Take that, Guthrie!" I made a fist and held it in the air, basking in my triumph.

Danny sighed.

"So much for my feeling of ominous dread all night," I added, almost wistful.

"What do you mean?" he asked.

"When we first got here, I had this weird feeling, like something was going to happen. And then it did, but it didn't. So in the end, I was wrong." If I was totally honest, I was a little disappointed that it had been a hoax. I guess my intuition had been off the mark. It wouldn't be the first time.

"You're not mad?"

"Kind of," I bluffed.

"Hey, now. Bigfoot most definitely does exist around here, and I've seen one. But I was afraid we wouldn't see one tonight, so I sort of made sure we did." He tossed his head, shaking a lock of hair out of his face. It was like he did it on cue, as if he knew I couldn't be mad at someone who was working the cute so hard. I totally fell for it.

"All right." I said, my voice softening. "It was a fun night, that's for sure. If anyone asks, I can truthfully say you know how to show a girl a good time."

"That sounds acceptable."

"And now I can go home and tell everyone I saw Bigfoot." I took another bite of cupcake.

Danny laughed, and we continued back to the truck. "You could pretend it was real, and write the article as if it was. That'll score you a lot of points. Both with your readers and your boss."

"Already thought of that," I said happily. "The rest of the article is gonna be a snap!"

I got to the truck before Danny did, and I leaned against the back tire on the passenger side to knock some dirt off my Vans. As I finished up, I heard a rustle in the trees beyond the front of the truck. Another silly raccoon. But then the rustling noise got louder, and I distinctly heard the muffled cluck of a chicken. A *chicken*. In the woods?

I looked up in time to see a dark figure walking toward me. It was very large and was holding something under one arm. The looming shape appeared to be hairy. And it was breathing very loudly, like it had sprinted to the truck. It appeared that Danny's hired monster was still on the clock. Maybe that bundle tucked under his arm was his human clothes. But I still couldn't account for the chicken clucks.

"Okay, Danny. Once was enough. No need to overdo it," I stood with one hip thrust out in defiance. The thing kept coming toward me. "It's all good, mister," I said to the guy in the hairy suit. "I know you're a fake. Aren't you tired? You can go ahead and call it a night."

Still, it kept coming at me. It was close enough now that I could see its face. The beady black eyes were staring at my hands. Wow, I thought. That was a very convincing monster mask.

I recognized what was tucked under its arm. It was a chicken. Not just any chicken though—it was Beryl. My jaw dropped. The hairy guy kept staring at my hand, and I looked down to realize I was still holding one Hostess Cupcake.

"Oh, I get it," I said with smarm aplenty. "You're hungry! I can't say as I blame you, having been out in the cold all night." I took a step closer to him. "I tell you what. Let's make a deal."

I walked up to him and held out my cupcake. "I'll trade you this for the chicken."

In one swift, smooth move, the guy grabbed the cupcake from my hand and shoved my chicken at me. He stuffed the cupcake in his mouth, turned, and ran back into the trees. Well, that had been fun. Beryl squirmed under my arm, as she usually did. Welcome home, jailbird.

"Nice touch, Danny," I mocked as I turned around to glare at him. I expected him to be laughing at me, but his face was white as a sheet. He stared at my chicken.

"Uh," he mumbled.

"What, don't have anything to say this time? You should have called your guy to tell him he could go home early. But the chicken is a nice touch, I have to admit. Oh, let me guess! You stole her from my backyard earlier in the week as part of the plan for tonight!" But as I said the words, I knew they weren't true because Beryl had gone missing *before* I'd arranged to go on the stakeout. But whatever. I was so mad it didn't matter much right that moment.

"Uh," Danny stammered again, still not moving.

"Whatever," I mumbled, unimpressed. I was tired. "Where can I put this thing?" I held Beryl out in front of me like she was someone else's dirty socks.

Without saying a word, Danny took Beryl from me and put her in a crate in the bed of his truck. It was probably meant for dogs but was now holding my recaptured bandit chicken.

I turned to get in the truck. I wasn't in the mood to climb Mount Everest again, but I also wasn't in the mood to wait for Danny to open the door and launch me into the seat. I took one last breath of lower-altitude oxygen and hoisted myself up.

We drove down the road about a quarter mile before Danny finally broke the tense silence.

"So guess what," he said slowly. I looked at him, and even though the only light in the cab came from the dashboard, I could tell his face was still devoid of color.

"Are we meeting Bigfoot at your pool for a midnight swim and a nightcap? I am not going skinny-dipping with something that hairy. Probably clog the pool filter."

"No," he said slowly. "It's just ... that thing back there? Just now? That wasn't my friend."

I laughed again. "What are you saying?"

"At the cabin. That was my friend Tom; he works on the ranch with me. That back there," he pointed with his thumb to the road behind us, "was an actual Sasquatch."

"Yeah, right. That thing was as much a Sasquatch as my aunt Margaret is. She's pretty hairy, but she ain't no Bigfoot. Did you see that costume? It was totally fake! The fur was thinning in a few spots. And I definitely saw a zipper." I desperately wanted to remember seeing a zipper.

"You may want to do a DNA test on your aunt, then, because I'm one hundred percent serious when I tell you, that was not Tom. That was a real live Bigfoot."

Danny sure did sound sincere. Huh. I looked at him again; his face was long, and his expression was serious.

I made myself form the words I was not wanting to speak. "You mean..."

"Yes."

"I just gave my last cupcake..."

"Uh huh."

"To a real Sasquatch?"

"This is what I am saying."

"And Bigfoot gave me my chicken back."

"You *know* that chicken?" Danny jerked his thumb toward the back of the truck.

"Oh yes," I said. "Beryl went missing on Thursday from a locked chicken coop in my backyard. And now you're telling me Bigfoot has been partying with my chicken, and traded her back to me for a cupcake." It sounded ridiculous coming out of my mouth. "Beryl is so much trouble that not even Bigfoot wants her."

"Well..." Danny looked like he was trying to mentally calculate the square root of 4,379,563,402.

I shrugged. "At least he was polite." I had to give him credit for having manners.

"That's all you have to say?" Perhaps Danny was expecting me to be freaked out by having come in contact with a real live Bigfoot. Maybe I was supposed to shriek at the top of my lungs and then dramatically lose consciousness. Now that I thought about it, I guess it was weird that I was so calm. Until I thought it through a little further.

"No," I said.

I turned to face him, preparing my thoughts. Now his profile was lit by the instrument cluster in the dash, and I couldn't help staring at his lips. Such a distraction, those lips.

Oh yeah! Bigfoot. Okay. I took a deep breath and pressed on.

"First off, I don't believe that was Bigfoot. Even you agreed it would have been very unlikely for us to see one tonight. I can't explain the chicken, though. That part is supremely weird. But if that was a Bigfoot, why on earth didn't you do something? You had a gun for cripes' sake!" It was all too much for my brain to handle, and I felt a little light-headed. "I mean, he could have thrown me over his shoulder and taken off! Were you just going to stand there and wave politely?"

I thought of all the things I hadn't done with my life yet. The novel writing. Finding that one big love. Figuring out how to make a decent homemade pizza crust.

By this time we were approaching Danny's house, and he pulled over to park. He cut the engine, and the road in front of us went dark.

"Look," he said, turning toward me so we were face-to-face. He slid over to the middle of the seat, closing the gap between us. Now I was hyperventilating because of his closeness.

"I'm telling you, that thing was an actual, bona fide, real live Bigfoot. It was not a man in a suit. It does seem too good to be true, but—"

"Good is a relative term!" I exploded. "Good? That was not good!"

"Sure it was! You've got everything you need for your article, and then some. Now you have proof! Firsthand experience! And it should be noted that I was right behind you with the rifle the whole time. I couldn't get a good shot at him because you were blocking my line of fire. If he had tried anything, I would have rescued you. But see, it turned out okay! I told you they like cupcakes. They're hungry and curious. He probably thought you were cute." He sparkled those blue eyes at me and leaned closer. Then he looked away. "But I sure can't explain the chicken."

I let my eyes close. Oh. My. God. A real Bigfoot? Nope. No way. My breath quickened as I worked hard to continue to convince myself it had all been fake, and Danny was still avoiding coming clean about his set-up. I opened my eyes, and there were those lips again. What a great distraction. He was so close that I could have leaned over and kissed him. So I did. And I made this one count. Let's say I forgot about Bigfoot, at least for a little while.

He reached out a hand and gently placed it on the back of my head, and I started to think we were having a contest to see who could go the longest without stopping for air. I knew if we stayed like this too long the mood would change to something a little more serious, and I was not ready to have that happen in the cab of a big giant monster truck. That was a high schooler's game.

I slowly, finally, pulled away.

"What was that for?" he mumbled.

"It was a test," I mumbled back.

"Did I pass?"

"I think so." I leaned against the passenger door to get a good look at him, and took a deep breath. "Yup. Yes. You passed," I exhaled.

"Good." He smiled, slid back behind the wheel, and started his truck back up. "Let's get you and your chicken home," he said softly.

We were quiet for a while, as I was still trying to comprehend the events of the evening. When we pulled out onto the main highway, he finally spoke.

"What test did I pass, exactly?"

I sighed. "I was wondering why you'd kissed me back at the cabin. I thought maybe you did it to distract me from noticing that Bigfoot was your friend in a bear suit. I thought maybe a second try might help me get more clarity on the subject."

"I see," he said thoughtfully. "And you're sure I passed?"

"Not one hundred percent. I still don't believe it was real, so maybe *all* of this is just a distraction." I waved my hand at the inside of the truck, not sure what I was referring to.

"Beverley," he began.

"Nope, don't want to hear it. But you're right about one thing—at least I've got some great material for my article."

Out of the corner of my eye, I saw him shrug his shoulders. I shrugged mine, too.

"I do have one question for you, though," I added. It was time to lay it all out on the table.

"Oh yeah? What's that?"

"Were you by any chance on I-35, south of town this afternoon?" I squeezed my eyes shut, waiting for his answer. I didn't want to know, but I really wanted to know.

"Hmm," he pondered. "Let me think now."

The suspense was driving me crazy.

"Hmm," he said again.

"It should be pretty easy to remember. Unless you suffer from short-term memory loss."

He laughed. "No, I'm messing with you. I wasn't on I-35 at all today. Had stuff to do on the ranch. How come?"

"No reason," I said, relief seeping into my voice and combining with exhaustion. I saw him shake his head out of the corner of my eye.

Twenty minutes later he dropped me off at my house, rather than at the *Ledger* offices, after I assured him I could walk over the following morning to get my car. I thanked him again for the entertainment, and he handed over my chicken and gave me an almost chaste peck on the cheek. It was not fully chaste because I picked up a sultry undertone as his lips brushed against my skin. At least I think I did, and anyway. It felt good to imagine some non-chaste thoughts were in there somewhere.

I locked Beryl up with her friends, who didn't seem all that happy to have her home. Too bad. They were simply going to have to deal with the fact that their anarchistic leader had returned. For good this time—I'd make sure of it. As I shut the pen as tightly as I could, I suddenly had a disturbing thought.

Had Beryl gotten herself out of the pen, or had Bigfoot come to get her? Who was I securing the latch against, exactly?

"Oh man," I said to the backyard. "Nuh-uh." For my own peace of mind, I went with the explanation that Beryl had escaped on her own. But if Bigfoot got in once to steal my Beryl, then he could probably do it again and there wasn't much I could do to stop him.

I headed back into the house and locked everything up. The supplies from my date backpack were strewn across the kitchen table—the empty thermos and food bags, the breath mints, my reporter's notebook. For all the evening's excitement, I hadn't written a single thing. But I was confident I'd be able to recall the events from memory, since the image of handing a cupcake to Bigfoot was permanently recorded in my mind.

I got ready for bed and reflected on the evening. The kiss, the guy in the hairy suit, the return of the prodigal hen, and the fact that I hadn't gotten to finish my cupcakes. I went to bed with my stomach growling.

TWENTY-TWO

Sunday morning found me up early, having risen with my all-natural alarm clocks, aka the chickens. I went out to check the coop—it was still locked tight, and everyone was accounted for. Beryl seemed quieter than usual. Maybe she'd been humbled by her stint as a Bigfoot captive. Perhaps she realized she was darn lucky not to have been eaten. It was possible she was even happy to be home. It was a stretch, but still possible.

I went for a short run—to retrieve my car. I had a shower and a small breakfast, and after drinking an obscenely large amount of coffee, I got to work on the Bigfoot article, which was due by six that evening. It went faster than I'd thought; everything suddenly had come together, once I'd spent a night out in the wilderness. I'd seen something firsthand, although I still wasn't convinced what it had been. In any case, I'd been scared out of my wits. Scared enough to write my very first Bigfoot investigative journalism piece.

The words flowed, and I wrote them down as they came. Even the title seemed to write itself: *AREA BIGFOOT SIGHTINGS LEAVE BIG IMPRESSION ON LOCALS.* I was finally channeling my inner Guthrie resident. Everything might work out, after all. I was done by noon.

After reading it through several times, I shut my eyes and hit Send, zapping the email off to Mark. I felt a huge wave of relief wash over me. It was over. I knew I might have more unusual assignments in the future, but I was glad this one was over with. And I hoped that now I'd be able to steer clear of Bigfoot for good. I checked my phone—I had just enough time to eat a little lunch, bake a cheesecake, and take a nap before Kelly's barbecue.

Around 2:00 p.m., my phone buzzed. It was a text from Mark. My stomach tightened—he usually only texted with bad news, like to give me a thirty-minute window to write a story about embezzlement in the Guthrie Ski Club, or something equally as scandalous. With trepidation, I peeked at the text.

Mark: *good job*.

I gasped. This was high praise, coming from him! I thought about texting him back with, *Are you sure? Because I was kind of scared that you wouldn't like it and then fire me, but please don't because I want to keep this job and I tried as hard as I could.* But then I thought better of it and decided not to write back at all. Yeah. The less said, the better.

Maybe I was finally making some headway, I thought, as I pulled a perfectly baked cheesecake out of the oven. Maybe I could get the hang of this small-town journalism thing, and maybe I could be part of the community after all. Maybe it was easier than I'd made it out to be.

With the scent of freshly baked dessert wafting through the house, I collapsed on the couch and immediately fell asleep. I did have the presence of mind to set an alarm on my phone before I crashed, but even so it was a miracle that I managed to be awake, showered, and dressed by the time my doorbell rang at 5:30.

"Hiya," Danny said as I opened the door. "Wow. You look great."

I peered down at my white T-shirt, cuffed jeans, and sockless feet nestled in my favorite pair of Vans. Hmm. Maybe my nap refreshed me to the point of looking fabulous, because even though I thought Vans and jeans looked spiffy, they hardly counted as great. Well, I'd take what I could get. Maybe he just liked Vans. I felt myself blushing, and suddenly I was tongue-tied. "Me too," I blurted out. "I mean, you do. Wait." Maybe I'd needed a longer nap.

He laughed and stepped into the house. "Are you ready to go?"

"Almost. I need to get the dessert," I said over my shoulder as I walked to the kitchen to grab the cheesecake. When I came back into the living room, he was still standing by the door, looking at my wall of bookshelves. "Ready," I said as I walked up beside him. I handed him the plate and ushered him back through the front door as I picked up the bag containing beer.

"How did the article turn out?" he asked.

I locked the door and gave him a sassy look. "You'll have to wait until next week's newspaper comes out, like everyone else."

"I figured you'd say something like that."

"Don't drop that cake."

We drove to Kelly's in his giant monster truck and spent the evening in her backyard with our friends. The food was delicious, the weather was flawless, and everyone was in a good mood—even Mark. The sun went down, and we continued to lounge outside, enjoying the ideal late-summer evening. In a matter of weeks, the breeze would turn cold and the leaves would begin to drop, signaling the coming of fall and winter. But for now, for this one warm, perfect evening, we silently acknowledged this fleeting moment of perfection. My shoulders relaxed, and I could feel a sense of relief washing over me. It was as if the stress from the past week melted off my body all at once. It was over.

I was still terrified of Bigfoot, and I probably always would be. But I'd faced my fear, found my lost chicken, and all that had happened was I'd lost a cupcake. I'd even met a nice guy.

I watched Danny as he talked with Ben about some kind of sportsing event. He took a swig of his beer and looked over at me. We shared a moment. Yes, he had been a definite highlight in a truly weird, stressful week.

Maybe I was finally settling in, or maybe life just seemed that much sweeter after surviving a face-to-face encounter with a cupcake-eating beast. At the moment, none of it mattered much.

I looked up at the sky and saw stars between the tree branches, and my breath caught. Suddenly I had an answer to that question I'd been asking myself for the last few months. Now I was totally and completely sure why I'd moved back to Oklahoma and made my home in Guthrie. As I sat with my friends, laughter sweeping across the yard on the warm breeze, the answer was clear. I'd found my place.

NEXT IN THE SERIES

Beverley Green's First Territorial Christmas

A lighthearted story about a grinch who's soon to discover the upside of the holiday season!

Enjoy the heck out of the holidays and pick up *Beverley Green's First Territorial Christmas* at your favorite retailer!

BOOKS BY ANDREA C. NEIL

THE BEVERLEY GREEN ADVENTURES

Beverley Green's First Adventure

Beverley Green's First Territorial Christmas

Beverley Green Finds True North

Beverley Green Comes Home

The Guthrie Short Stories

OLD SCHOOL MYSTERIES

The Blingsters

The Big Cheese

Gone Grandpa

The Last Resort

MICRO FICTION

Days Are Beautiful: 100 flash fiction stories

No Surprises: 100 flash fiction stories

Visit acneil.com to receive a free story

ACKNOWLEDGMENTS

Thanks to:

Marcus for all the cappuccinos and for keeping my feet on the ground.

My Wise Aunt Deepti for all the encouragement and project management skillz.

Michele Chiappetta, the fearless editor who went through a lot of red pens on this one.

Ren and Dayl – the best dang friends a weirdo could have.

Cynthia - thank you for bringing Beverley, Beryl, and Bigfoot to life through your amazing artwork.

The Beverley Beta Readers - Hope, Alan, Erika, Susan, Keith, Mary, and Deepti - thanks for feedback on this new version of an old story! Your time and insights are appreciated.

My mom and my dad ... because parents.

And to all the Unicorns out there–yeah, that's you–keep on being your amazing self.

ABOUT THE AUTHOR

Andrea lives in Oklahoma but grew up in Southern California —and the latter will always be home in her heart. In 2015 she left a job in finance to follow her passion for writing and creating art. With age comes wisdom, or at least a few more stories to tell, and in 2018, Andrea began self-publishing quirky novels with the intention of brightening her readers' day. When she's not trying to get her own words onto a page, Andrea edits other people's writing, eats dark chocolate, and goes on walks if the weather's nice.

acneil.com

amazon.com/author/andreaneil

bookbub.com/profile/andrea-c-neil

facebook.com/andreacneil

instagram.com/andreacneil

Made in the USA
Monee, IL
10 February 2025

11810201R00135